# An Alpha's Path

## A Redwood Pack Novella

### By
### CARRIE ANN RYAN

# An Alpha's Path

Melanie is a twenty-five year old chemist who has spent all of her adult life slaving at school. With her PhD in hand, she's to start her dream job, but before she does, her friend persuades her to relax and try to live again. A blind date set up through her friends seems like the perfect solution. Melanie can take one night away from the lab and let her inner vixen out on a fixed blind date — a chance to get crazy with a perfect stranger. The gorgeous hunk she's to meet exceeds her wildest dreams — be he is more than what he appears and Melanie's analytical mind goes into overdrive.

Kade, a slightly older werewolf (at over one hundred years), needs a night way from the Pack. Too many responsibilities and one near miss with a potential mate made Kade hide in his work, the only peace he can find. His brother convinces him to meet the sexy woman for a one night of fun. What could it hurt? But when he finds this woman could be his mate, can he convince her to leave her orderly, sane world and be with him and his wolf-half, for life?

# Dedication

This novel wouldn't have happened without a push from Rebecca Royce. She gave me the edge I needed to put my thoughts on paper. Thank you.

My romance critters are a group of amazing people who held my hand and gave me their shoulders when I need a good cry. Specifically Leia, Gina and Lia. Y'all rock. To those of you who inked my paper, you know who you are – thank you.

Finally, to my hubby. Thanks for sitting with me on the couch when I needed company and stuck on a chapter. Love you.

# CHAPTER 1

The thundering in Melanie Cross's ears increased as her breath became shallow. Palms sweaty, she bit her lip and nervously tapped her foot, as she took in her surroundings. The lobby looked like a palace. Tall, cream colored pillars and chocolate molding surrounded the opulent sitting area. Gorgeous light fixtures with tear drop crystals hung from the walls and the ceiling, giving the room a soft glow. Warm and inviting. But she didn't want to feel invited. She wanted to leave. Run away and never look back.

What was she thinking? Melanie was a smart, hardworking person. A freshly printed PhD in Nuclear Chemistry and a painstakingly long, nine hundred page, leather bound thesis sat on her desk, proved it. She could accomplish things on her own. Her ideas were acclaimed, and her work referenced numerous times. Any job her heart desired, now hers for the asking. Because of this she was about to bypass the normal post-doc route of working underneath yet another professor. Now she would be an Associate

Professor with her own research group at an Ivy League University.

She gained a few close friends over the years, and even though she didn't have an overly active social life – okay she didn't have one to speak of – she thought her life was just peachy.

Yet her friends thought with all of the accomplishments in her educational career she was still uptight. Some even said she was missing her ideal husband. But her closest friend Larissa decided she just needed to get laid.

Mel thought back to when her best friend first told her this crazy idea.

"Really Melanie, when was the last time you got laid? First year? Even earlier? It's ridiculous! You are practically a born-again virgin." Larissa laughed at her own joke and then slid a business card across her newly cleared off lab bench.

"What's this?" A name printed on the card, Jamenson Services, stared back at her. "You're sending me to a gigolo?" She gasped and tried to throw the card away before Larissa quickly swiped it from her hands.

"No. The Jamensons are contractors. The man who owns it is an acquaintance of mine. He built the new green house at my parents. Come on, you need a date and so does he. It is only for one evening, and sex isn't required. But honestly, the way those Jamenson boys are built, you'll be dropping your panties at his command," Larissa lifted one eyebrow and laughed again.

"Oh I don't think so. I'm not that desperate. It's just that I've been so focused on my work that I didn't have time to date a man, let alone look for one." Melanie knew she could've just looked across the lab bench for the last five years to find a date. But really Timmy wasn't at all that worth to look at.

"Honey, you are too rigid. You need one night off before you skip ahead to the next part of your life. Call the number on the card and talk to Jasper. He's the brother of the guy I think would be perfect for you. Do it and get laid." She laughed, pushing the card in Melanie's hand.

Somewhere deep down Melanie knew Larissa was right. Melanie didn't throw the card away. She couldn't. Now six weeks later, she found herself sitting in the Hilton Resort in Seattle, about to vomit on the new black Fuck-Me pumps Larissa forced her to wear.

"Miss? Are you okay?"

At the sound of a deep voice, her head shot up to look at a very handsome man. Dark skinned, with piercing eyes, he surveyed her. *Oh my, is this her date?*

"Oh I'm fine. Just getting the nerve to walk into the bar, to get even more nerve to wait for my date." She winced at how fast and squeaky she spoke but really – why was she even here?

"I'm the manager, Lance Morse, let me walk you to the bar, and get you a shot of that nerve." He winked and she smiled him.

Melanie took a deep breath. "Okay." Wow. Surely, anyone could tell she was *Dr.* Melanie Cross, rather than the dumb blonde she seemed to be portraying. *Or not.*

He took her arm and guided her away from where she sat for twenty minutes regretting her decisions. Lance walked her toward the bar, while talking about the various hotel and resort amenities and events. She nodded while he spoke, as she felt the bar beckon her.

"Here we are. Thank you again for coming. If you need anything, feel no hesitation in asking one of my employees to assist you or ask for me by name. Enjoy your evening, Melanie Cross."

She smiled then stopped breathing for a moment. "How..."

"Your friend, Larissa, texted me earlier to be on the lookout for a small, shy blonde by the name of Melanie Cross and you seemed to fit the description. I took a gamble." He smiled.

Before she could respond, he winked again and walked out of the bar leaving her alone.

As she sat down, a Bay Breeze magically appeared in front of her and the bartender winked at her as he walked away. Did all men at this hotel wink? Her phone buzzed as she was just about to get freaked out.

*Melanie babe, please relax. Your date should be there soon. Take a nice drink of that concoction and enjoy your evening. Oh and get laid.*

Melanie laughed. Larissa possessed a one-track mind. She took a drink when her phone buzzed again.

*Just remember to keep an open mind. He really is quite sweet and won't bite. Well, only occasionally. And only if you want him to.*

What the hell?

\*\*\*\*

Kade Jamenson stepped into the lobby and was immediately assaulted by the delicate honey vanilla scent wafting throughout the room. His muscles clenched and he balled his fists, gaining control.

*Mate?*

4

He tried to tone down his edginess, but it felt as though his wolf was trying to claw his way out from the inside.

He spoke to the wolf inside his head, *"It surely smells like a possibility. But we are here for a date with a human. I am not so callous as to stand up a perfectly reasonable date just so I can follow a scent that could lead to disaster. Let me figure out this date first and then I will follow the scent if we have to. We already made the mistake of the wrong mate once; I don't want to do it again."*

*Mate!*

His wolf was right. He knew the woman who could be his mate wasn't even in the room, yet her scent and the urge to join with another was stronger by far than with Tracy. Kade took a deep breath of the honey vanilla scent and his balls tightened.

Damn. This woman was potentially his mate. How could this happen the night he finally took up his brother Jasper's offer of a blind date?

He quickly texted Jasper to let him know that he needed to break his date or do some major rescheduling and thinking. He couldn't be respectful to this human woman if he was aroused by another scent. It wasn't fair to any party.

His phone buzzed not one minute later with a response.

*Kade, don't be an ass. Just go meet Melanie and I am sure you will have your answers.*

After that cryptic comment, Kade didn't know what to think. Jasper told him, Melanie was a 5'2" petite blonde who should fit against his 6'2" frame nicely. Those liquid brown eyes that gazed up at him from her photograph, made him want to know what was behind them. That was a first for him. He might have been slightly nervous about the date but he was oh so willing and eager to meet with her. Just remembering her photo made him smile and want to see her in person. He was an Alpha male with no small amount of pride. Hell, he was the Heir to the Redwood Pack, first in line to the throne. Kade took one last deep breath of that honey vanilla scent and squared his shoulders.

He had a date with a pretty blonde.

# CHAPTER 2

M elanie sat at her table and checked her watch. He was only three minutes late. That didn't mean he was going to stand her up. Right? He just wasn't a perpetually early person like her. It wasn't evidence that they weren't compatible.

Compatible? Gawd. She needed another drink. This was just for one night. One night only – if he even showed.

She let out a deep breath and was about to order another drink when she caught sight of an absolutely gorgeous specimen of man.

His body towered over six feet with wide shoulders and a trim waist. The kind of guy displayed on one of those silly romance novel covers. Dark brown, almost black hair, that barely reached his shoulders begged for her hands to tangle in those silky looking strands. A few luscious locks fell into his eyes.

*Those eyes.*

Deep green eyes set under dark lashes. Pools of jade, swallowing her whole. They were piercing and shifted throughout the room, taking in his surroundings. Yet it felt as though he never let his eyes leave her. *Oh my.* Mel fanned her face before blushing when she realized what she was doing. Damn he was beautiful.

He practically prowled through the room drawing the attention of almost every woman and even some of the men. An almost animalistic wave of seduction ebbed from him.

*Damn.*

Please, if there was a God, let this be the mysterious Kade Jamenson. *Please.* Larissa didn't give her a picture or description of his looks as she said it would ruin the moment of first meeting. Melanie hadn't agreed when she read that, but if this were Kade she would take back anything bad she ever thought about her best friend.

His nostrils flared as if he were taking in a deep breath, then he smiled a truly feral and triumphant smile as he came to the head of her table.

"Melanie?"

"Kade?"

The both laughed quietly at the sound of them talking at once.

"Would you like to take a seat?" She was the one who spoke first. Well, the alcohol must have gone straight to her head because that never happened with men. Especially drop dead gorgeous men.

He smiled again and sat down gracefully in the seat across from her. She could've melted on the spot under the intensity of his gaze.

"Yes, I am Kade Jamenson. It is good to meet you Melanie Cross." The way her name roughly rasped through his sensuous lips sent shivers through her. "May I order you another drink?"

It took her a moment to drag her eyes from his lips to answer. "No. No, I'm fine at one drink. It seems to have gone straight to my head." She could feel the heat creeping toward her cheeks as she shyly bowed her head. Gawd, why not just tell him you are a lightweight before he takes you up to have wild and steamy sex?

Well, she guessed that didn't sound so horrible. Exciting, but not horrible.

He laughed at her remark. "Sounds reasonable, water it is. Then how about we order something to eat while we talk and get to know one another. I don't know about you but I was nervous as hell before I walked into the bar and saw you across the tables." He shook his head and chuckled under his breath "I know I shouldn't say that because now you think I am some loser, but I can honestly say I'm not nervous anymore. I'm happy I said yes to this date." He smiled at her just as the waiter came to take their order. "Ladies first."

"Um. Okay." She stumbled a bit as she opened her menu. Try as she might, she couldn't get her hands to stop shaking. It's been so long since she's been out. But none of those other dates could have prepared her for the example of sexiness sitting across from her. She sighed inwardly. *He is knock-dead gorgeous.*

Melanie quickly glanced down at the menu and chose the first thing that seemed edible. "I will have the Glazed Apricot Chicken with sautéed green beans and a side salad with balsamic vinaigrette dressing please. Oh, and another glass of water please." The waiter nodded while he took her order and menu before turning his attention to Kade.

"I will have the porterhouse – rare." Kade smiled at himself, as if what he said was funny. "Also a baked potato with the works. Thank you." He gave the waiter his menu. "Would you like to start off with an appetizer, Melanie?" His eyes implored her to do whatever he wanted. She shook her head to rid it of that odd and irritable notion.

"No, I think my dinner will suffice. I suppose you're a meat and potato type of guy since you didn't even bother with a vegetable." She shut her mouth quickly with an audible snap.

"Sorry. That isn't any of my business. Eat what you want. I'm going to shut up now." Her face was so warm that if her cheeks were any redder she would be a tomato.

Kade just threw his head back and laughed loudly, drawing the attention of a few of the nearby tables.

"Don't worry. Say whatever is on your mind. I don't think we need to keep secrets from each other." An odd flash of something passed over his eyes, but he quickly hid it. "But yes, I seem to be a meat and potatoes kind of guy. I'm not a huge fan of rabbit food and tend not to order it if I don't have to. It just seems like such a waste."

"Oh."

Oh yeah. That PhD was really shining through her vocabulary tonight.

"So tell me about yourself, Melanie Cross." He took a drink of the water in front of him and leaned toward her as if he didn't want to miss a thing she was saying. "Jasper told me some things, but that was just facts and figures. I want to know more about you and learn it from you." From the way he looked at her, he must be serious.

"Well, I'm sure you got most of this from your brother, but here it goes. I'm a twenty-five year old single chemist. I just finished my thesis and am on a break before I start my next job. I've spent way too much time behind a lab bench, with my nose in chemical journals to date properly according to my friends. Hence, the seemingly last ditch effort in

relationships known as a blind date. So here I am."
She spoke so fast that she sounded almost shrill and
defensive. But she was terrified of what was supposed
to take place that evening – even if according to her
friend she didn't have to see his face after tonight.
Although, with a face like that, it was unlikely that she
would ever forget it.

"So what about you?" She wanted the spotlight off
herself as soon as possible. For a woman who could
talk in front of four hundred chemistry freshman or
seven of the meanest and smartest professors in the
field without breaking a sweat, she was slowly going
crazy and incomprehensible sitting in front of this one
man. One very hot man.

"Well, I'm a contractor and architect outside the
Seattle area. I live near my family and we like the
woods, and lack of crowds and large population noise.
I own a contracting company and mostly build
residential and small businesses. Sometimes I do
special projects, like you friend's parents' greenhouse.
I don't date all that much because I too am busy with
work. I was seeing a woman for... a bit before we
broke it off." His face didn't reveal anything but she
thought she saw an odd expression flicker across his
eyes before he blinked it away.

"Was it serious?" She couldn't believe out of all
the things he said that was the one thing that popped
into her mind. And frankly, did she even want to
know? This was a first date for crying out loud.

"It could have been, but it just didn't work out.
She is with someone else, and I am free to pursue
other... avenues." He kept pausing before some words
as if he were trying to decide what to say – as if he
were keeping a secret from her. *Hmm...*

"I'm glad, however, that things took this turn
because now I'm on a date with a lovely woman." He

flashed her a wicked smile right as the waiter brought their entrees.

"Enjoy your meal, Melanie, even though you have more rabbit food than meat."

She laughed, enjoying his odd sense of humor. They quieted while they began to eat.

\*\*\*\*

A few bites in, Kade noticed that Melanie barely touched her food. Nervousness emanated from her skin. Fear even. He, on the other hand, fought his wolf to tone down their hunger for something other than their meal.

The honey vanilla scent sat across from him. His wolf was beyond pleased and ready to jump across the table and mount her.

The man however, was a little more cautious. Relief flooded him when the sweet honey vanilla scent radiated from the beautiful goddess from the photograph. He was on a blind date with his future mate. *How fucking awesome was that?*

His brother and Larissa were either sneaky geniuses or very lucky. They both were scary beyond all recognition sometimes, but amazing nonetheless. He owed the matchmaking duo an apology, but later. First, he had to get to know Melanie and get her upstairs. Even if they didn't have sex tonight and only talked, he would be fine. Because they would have hundreds of years to get to the dirty fun part.

And yes, she was his mate. The mating urge rode him harder than anything he ever felt. Kade was not letting this one get away. He'd do anything in his power to make the blond pixie in front of him want to spend the rest of her soon-to-be-long life with him.

With that goal in place, his wolf subsided a bit. *Don't screw this up. This is the one, Kade.*

Kade just smiled at his wolf and brought his attention back to his date.

"Are you done eating? Or would you like some more time?"

She bowed her head again, as a cute and damn sexy blush rose to her cheeks. He wondered if she blushed like that everywhere. She was wearing a sexy black silk and lace number that only accentuated her slightly curvy figure. She was a tiny thing that he knew could fit against him just right.

He could only imagine how she would look with her pale, creamy skin against his darker, bronze skin. Watching her lashes brush her cheeks as she glanced down at her barely touched meal he knew he wanted to kiss any fears or anxiety she carried away.

*Mate? I think it's time to go upstairs. Don't you?*

He couldn't agree more with his wolf. But he didn't want to rush her. No matter what happened tonight, they would be going upstairs – that was a guarantee. What they did once they arrived however – was up to the woman in front of him.

"You look as if you have the same appetite as me." At the sound of his voice, her head popped up from whatever deep thoughts she was thinking. "What do you say we take a walk around the property?"

"Oh, okay. I guess I am just not that hungry tonight." She smiled sheepishly as she set down her fork and any pretense of enjoying her food.

"Let's go then, the check is taken care of, so we can take our time tonight."

13

She smiled timidly again and grabbed her wrap and black, beaded bag. He fluidly rose from his seat and offered her his hand.

"Where would you like to walk to?" Kade, again, toned down his wolf and waited for Melanie's reply.

"Our room?"

Her face was still stunning with the shade of beet red it became at her surprising, yet not unwelcome, announcement.

His wolf growled in agreement and preened for attention.

He gave her a smile that promised sinful and wicked deeds.

"That sounds like an outstanding idea, Melanie."

# CHAPTER 3

Kade led her toward the elevator through the atrium, with his hand against the small of her back. The warmth of her delicate body radiated through her thin dress and with his wolf senses, he felt her heart pounding and her breath coming in almost shallow pants. She was aroused, but also succumbing to nerves and fear, the scent wafting from her skin. The need to reassure her pounded through his body, and even though his wolf practically begged to have her, he agreed.

Kade clasped her small, silky soft hand in his larger, more calloused one and entwined their fingers together before giving it a comforting squeeze. Mel smiled up at him and warmth bloomed in his chest. She was so small, so fragile. His.

The elevator chimed and a couple walked out. They exuded sex and drowsiness, and he wasn't the least bit jealous. He was about to be in the same room as his mate.

As the elevator rode up to the twenty-first floor, he tried to make small talk but neither of them was interested. He chuckled under his breath, feeling like a teenager again. Too bad it was almost a hundred years since he was one.

They finally entered their room, aptly named the Dreams Room and closed the door with a resounding click behind them. The room was draped in white and cream silks. There were linens surrounding the open and airy bedroom with candles barely lit where the linens gaped open. The bed was almost bare except for fluffy white pillows and a luscious white comforter. That was good; he didn't want his claws, if they did make an appearance, to destroy too much.

Once they both took in their surroundings, Kade led Melanie toward the center where she abruptly halted and turned around.

Her eyes were huge and she was barely breathing when she spoke hurriedly.

"I changed my mind. I don't think I can do this. I mean it's not you. It's me. Oh hell!" She slapped her hand to her forehead then covered her eyes. Kade bit the inside of his cheek to stop from laughing. She was really too cute with her deep blush and the way she bit into her plump lip.

"I mean, you are great looking. Fabulous in fact. But I'm sure you know that. You must have woman throwing themselves at your feet in droves, but I don't think I can do this. I don't know why I even signed up for this, let alone tell you we should come up to the room." If she continued to talk, she would rationalize herself right out of the room and out of his life. His wolf and he snorted silently. *Yeah, like that's going to happen.*

"Melanie. Calm down. It's okay. We have this room, but nowhere does it say we need to utilize it doing any acrobatics. Well I guess we can try to do cartwheels and those backhand flip spring things that gymnasts do but I don't think that is required either. If you want to talk, we can just do that."

A look mixed of laughter, relief and disappointment ran across her face. Damn, her face was expressive. When they finally did go to bed together, he was going to love watching new emotions run across her face when she came.

It was her disappointment he needed to address first. One giant step and he could crush his body to hers and feast on her until she came. His blood pulsed through his veins, and he held himself still so he wouldn't shake with desire. He had to reassure her that she wasn't the least bit unwanted.

"Now don't look at me like that," Kade's wolf growled at the thought. Fuck, if she gave the okay, he would be on top of her, his cock encased in her pussy in a heartbeat. She was fucking jaw-dropping. "If you were to say 'let's go for it' right now, then I would be there because believe me, you are sexy and I do want you. But I also don't want to do anything that would scare you or that you are not ready for. We can just talk or watch a movie. We can even go for that walk we discussed but opted out of. I am really enjoying getting to know you, and I don't want this night to end just yet."

Kade took a tentative step toward her and removed her wrap and purse to place on the couch in the corner before taking her hand in his.

"I have an idea. Why don't you go take a bath and relax? I promise I won't enter the room - unless you ask for me." A sly smile lifted the corners of his mouth as he kissed her palm. Her skin was warm against his lips. "Once you're done, you can come back out and we can do whatever you want. No pressure." He spread out his hands to convey his easy going attitude and gave her his best innocent expression.

For a moment, she didn't look like she believed his face or his body language, but the words may have made a tiny chink in her armor.

"No pressure? I don't think that will happen. But a bath does sound decadent. It's been awhile since I've taken a long, relaxing soak." Her eyes brightened more and more as the idea took hold.

"Okay then, when you're in there I'm going to order us some snacks and see what they have for movies. We can just veg out and get to know each other some more."

Her answering smile could've blinded some men. "That sounds like a fabulous idea."

She picked up her larger bag that the bellhop brought up earlier and gave him one last smile before heading to the bathroom and shutting the door softly.

Kade took a deep breath of her honey vanilla scent that was more concentrated in the enclosed room and almost shook with anticipation.

He practically glided to the phone to place their orders and smiled to himself. The night may not be exactly how he expected so far, but he wouldn't want to lose a single moment of time with his mate.

****

Melanie took a deep breath as she gave herself a good look in the mirror. This bathroom may be the greatest and most luxurious thing she'd ever seen, but she barely gave it a second glance.

What the hell was she doing? There was a gorgeous god standing in the room that she practically ran from. What the hell was she doing in here?

18

All throughout dinner, she couldn't seem to string two coherent sentences together. She resembled a ditzy, shy deer in the headlights. It was no wonder Kade was just fine with not having sex tonight. Oh, he may have said that he wanted her, but he didn't seem to fight for it.

Oh, that was just great. Kade was considerate of her feelings, yet here she was, making him the bad guy. This whole experience made her a wreck. Maybe Mel wasn't experienced with men, but she was experienced with meeting people and communicating with another human being. Tonight was a once in a lifetime opportunity to have wild and passionate sex with a near stranger. And oh yes, just looking at Kade, she knew it would be exactly that. She grew damp just thinking about him, and what wicked things could await her if she would just say yes.

And honestly, what was stopping her? Going through with this would leave her with an amazing and glorious memory. She needed more of those. The need to hear she was beautiful, sexy and wanted overwhelmed her. Mel didn't want to be the "smart" one anymore. She squared her shoulders and looked at herself in the mirror once more.

Oh yes. Once through that door, the needy and long ignored woman in her was going to go out there and tell Kade to fuck her. It was what she wanted – what she needed.

Mel took a steadying breath and changed into more comfortable attire. Comfort wasn't to be found in that slinky dress and Fuck-Me heels. If she were going to make a new memory, she was going to damn well do it in an outfit she liked. Grabbing the door handle with a firm grip, she thought about what was beyond it. The passage led to maybe not her destiny but definitely an amazing night.

# CHAPTER 4

Kade looked over his shoulder as the bathroom door opened. Melanie changed into a new more comfortable outfit. The top and leggings she put on did little to hide her delicious curves and only increased his desire for her. "Decided against the bath?" Kade's breath became shallow as he watched Melanie practically prowl toward him, even as his eyebrow slightly lifted.

"Uh huh. I also decided that you sounded like a much better way to pass the time and relax me than taking a bath." She smiled a purely seductive grin, though he could still read the hesitancy in her eyes.

He took a steadying breath and nodded. Words seemed to fail him – and the wolf – at the moment.

Kade stepped toward her and brushed his knuckles against her cheek. The responding shiver brought his wolf back to attention.

"We still need to have our first kiss, Mel." Another half step and their bodies brushed, feather light. The anticipation of what was to come proving more erotic than he ever dreamed.

His fingertips traced across her eyebrow and down her cheek before resting on her lips. They were silky and smooth. The tip of her tongue tentatively slipped out to lick his finger, and he moaned.

Leaning forward, he brushed his lips against hers, so lush and ripe he almost came right there. His body melted against hers, losing himself until there was no division between them. Her taste fuzzed his brain, he was slowly losing it. But what the hell, this was his mate, and this was their first kiss.

It was a kiss so sweet and so promising that the sexual tension seemed to hum throughout the room.

He licked the seam of her lips, and she opened for him and moaned. *Dear God, that honey vanilla would kill him.* His other arm came up from behind, and he dug his fingers in her hair in a gentle yet possessive grip. *Mine.*

When they finally broke apart, they were both breathless, and the corner of his mouth lifted.

\*\*\*\*

Kade's arm wrapped around her as he slowly and methodically ran his hand up and down her back. Shivers of need racked her body. *Oh my, he's amazing.* He led her toward the bed and sat her down gently before joining her. His warmth brushed against her skin through the thin peasant blouse she wore. Another ache ran down her spine, and she took a deep breath and inhaled his scent. Masculine pine and forest invaded her senses, causing her head to swim. She wanted to taste him again. Mel wasn't so hesitant and scared anymore. Well, maybe it was a new scared, but she was anxious to see what came of it.

Kade's hand brushed the underside of her breast and her breath caught. Goosebumps rose in the wake of his hand as it slid down to cup her bottom. She snuggled closer into to him and moved her hand onto his chest in small circles. His heartbeat under her palm increased and his breath quickened. Mel raised her head to look up at him – his pupils dilating in his forest green eyes.

"I'm glad that you decided against the walk." His voice had deepened and taken a rougher edge to it – almost a growl.

The rough tips of his fingers walked against her skin as his hand brushed underneath her shirt. A gasp escaped her, as she felt them splay against her back. Kade lowered his head and captured her lips. His tongue ran the seam of her lips and she parted them. He kissed her fiercely before moving his lips to her chin and then kissing a trail down the center of her chest. His mouth reached her breast and he clamped his lips on her nipple through her shirt. A moan tore from her throat, before she let him strip off her blouse. His tongue delved into her mouth with fevered passion. He undid the front clasp of her bra and her breasts released heavy and ready. Kade went back to her mouth and kissed her deeply. She gasped into his mouth and arched against him. Her nipple pebbled against his touch and she shuddered again.

Kade continued to devour her mouth as he kneaded her breast. She ran her free hand up his chest and neck and dug her fingers into his hair and scalp. He released her mouth and Mel groaned. A soft laugh left his lips before he kissed under her jaw and traced a fiery path down her neck and then back up to nibble on her ear. Her breath came in short pants as she felt his heated breath whisper against her and she moaned.

Her lover moved her body so she lay down, all the while touching her. He rested between her legs and bent down to look directly in her eyes. His pupils were so deep with desire that she could only see a small rim of green. For a moment, she thought they glowed but it must have been a trick of light. She arched against him and ran her foot across his calf. He swallowed hard and bent to capture her lips again, kissing her fully and then lowered to kiss her chin, her neck, and collarbone.

He went back to her breasts, scraping his teeth against the rosy flesh. Mel gasped and moved against him. Kade pulled her nipple through his teeth and suckled before biting down. He released her and then laved the sting. Shudders racked her as he turned his attention to her other nipple and repeated the process. Her desire pooled deep inside her womb and she clenched her legs around Kade trying to ease the ache. A deep masculine chuckle vibrated against her, and he moved downward to kiss her belly slowly. Moving further down, he ran his tongue against the top of her leggings. She moaned and tried to wrap her legs around him but he steadied her. His hands glided up her legs to the waist band and began to pull her leggings down. Mel lifted her bottom to allow him easier access. Kade groaned and pulled them completely off, staying on his knees a moment longer to look his fill up her body as she lay wanton before him. He lowered himself and placed his mouth directly on her pussy through her black, silk panties. Kade breathed in and suckled her clit and she came without his direct touch on her skin. The landscape shattered beneath her eyelids while stars blanketed her vision, and she screamed and moaned. He twisted his hands in the sides of her panties and lowered them slowly down her legs, climbing back quickly and parted her legs wider. He sat back on his haunches to gaze at her. Mel blushed, feeling open and awkward under his scrutiny.

"Your pink flesh is glistening for me, Mel. You are so beautiful when you come and I want to see it again." As he spoke, her muscles relaxed, tension easing from her body. "This bud is waiting for my mouth. Do you want me to suck your clit, Melanie? Do you want me to lick your seam and fill your pussy with my fingers?"

Mel wasn't capable of speaking, so she simply nodded. A satisfied smile spread over his face, and he lowered his head to blow across her. His cool breath dancing against her warmth, made her moan again.

"Damn, I'm going to feast on you until you come, and then I'm going to eat you again. You taste like ripe strawberries ready for plucking. And I'm going to pluck and suck you until I drain you dry of every last juice. Your juices are going to run down my chin and then I am still not going to have my fill of you."

Then he licked her from seam to clit and bit gently down when he reached her nub. Mel practically buckled off the bed and he pressed his arms against her hips to keep her placed where he wanted her. His tongue lapped up her juices, and then she felt him enter one finger insider her. Mel's inner walls clamped down on his finger.

"God, Melanie. You are so tight. I can't wait until I can fill you with my cock and you can milk me. Move on me, ride my hand. Oh Melanie, baby, yeah you like that don't you?" He returned to feast on her and she came again. But he didn't stop this time as she rode her climax and began to feel the next crest on its way. He entered a second, then a third finger, and worked her pussy while his mouth was still savoring and devouring. She looked down to see his dark hair against her pale skin and smiled. He licked her again and then placed a kiss on either side of her thighs before coming up and kissing her.

She tasted herself on his tongue but didn't feel embarrassed. Mel didn't have enough energy to do so. Kade kissed the side of her mouth and then her temple before moving the blankets on top of them. He surrounded her with his body, and she felt his hot and throbbing cock against her hip, and she wondered why he didn't do anything about it.

"I can't even think Kade. Oh my God. I think I lost count of orgasms. But what about you?"

He laughed deeply against her and rubbed his hand against her side.

"I have an idea, why don't we take care of each other at the same time?"

Her gaze widened and she moaned. This man was going to be the death of her. "I have never done that before. Okay."

This new found sensuality in her must be a gift from Kade. She wasn't going to stop it yet. If ever.

He sat up on the bed and knelt before her. Mel did the same and unbuttoned and unzipped his jeans. Her eyes widened when his cock fell into her hands hard and ready.

"You aren't wearing any underwear. Bad boy." She got closer and licked the drop of pre cum at the head.

Kade groaned and forced her on her side. He then twisted her around so her head was at the edge of the bed then laid next to her on her other side.

Mel moaned out loud when he placed his lips directly on her clit. She was already wet and ready for him. He nipped the gentle skin of her inner thigh, then licked up her juices that ran down, escaping her heat.

Mel moaned his name and then placed her lips around his cock. He sucked her clit and worked his tongue in and out of her passage while caressing her ass and gripping her hips. The coarse hair at the base of his cock tickled her lips before she slowly licked her way up his dick to the head. Taking a breath, she put her mouth back on him, swallowed him whole, and rolled her tongue against him. He seemed to like that because he moaned and bit down on her clit in response. In turn, she moaned around his cock in an almost never ending circle of pleasure. She worked him with one hand while digging her other hand into the meaty flesh of his ass. Her throat contracted around his cock as she came. Sucking harder, she gripped him firmer and his balls drew tight.

"I'm about to drop a load down that pretty throat Mel. Are you going to be a good girl and swallow it all?" At her nod with his cock still in her mouth he continued, "Damn, swallow my seed and suck harder, Mel."

When she rubbed her clit against his face, he came in her mouth. She swallowed it all and he screamed her name.

When Kade's still hard cock slipped from her lips, she moaned. *Oh my. How could she already miss his taste?* He lifted her leg and twisted himself so he lay practically on top of her without resting any of his weight on her. *So considerate, her lover.*

\*\*\*\*

Kade's heaven resembled a blond goddess. Her sweet honey taste still flavored his tongue. Mel's soft, sated body lay beneath him, waiting for more. And oh, how he would deliver.

He spread her legs and positioned his cock against the entrance of her heat. Her eyes widened a bit and he kissed her slowly and longingly. His wolf was practically howling for him to turn her around and mount her. But the man wanted to see her face when he joined her for the first time.

He wouldn't claim her tonight. Not officially. A bite mark in the curve where her neck met her shoulder began the mating. But he would leave his scent on every square inch of her so no other wolf could come near her without knowing who she belonged to. In turn, her honey vanilla scent already seeped beneath his skin and he never wanted to wash it off. She may not know it yet, but she was doing some claiming of her own. The fact he didn't share with her what he was left him with guilt, but in time she would know the truth. He just hoped she would take it well.

"Wait, Kade. What about a condom?"

Mel's wide eyes forced Kade to stop, sweat dripping down his body.

*Shit. How did he explain his way out of this one?*

"Damn, I don't have anything with me. I don't have any diseases, I promise." His voice deepened with barely contained need.

"Me neither. And I'm on birth control."

The thought of Mel pregnant with their young almost sent him over the edge. Their future. Their legacy.

Not that it mattered, since he wouldn't mark her tonight so there would be no pups. Without the mark, they wouldn't be officially mated and therefore no children.

"Are you ready, Melanie?"

She nodded and he slowly entered her. *Fuck.* A soft velvet heat encased him. Kade thought he was going to die from the pleasure of it and he was only partially in. Slowly, he rocked in and out of her pussy before taking the final plunge and sheathed himself to the hilt.

Kade waited and didn't move for a moment while she adjusted to him. This was the first time that he had made love. Yes, he had fucked his share of women throughout his hundred or so years, but this was the first time he was making love with his mate. Bliss.

When she was ready, he slowly pulled out and then leisurely entered her again. She gasped and moaned while he did his best to maintain control. Wanting to take the first time slow, Kade paced himself. Going too fast, too soon might bring out his claws. There would be plenty of time later to go crazy and fuck her brains out. As it was, he had to make sure his eyes didn't glow when he came. Scaring her away wasn't an option.

He made love to her, kissed her and loved her. Murmuring her name against her skin sent shivers down the both of them. His wolf came to the surface as he rode her harder, an outcome that could not be avoided. Kade quickly hid his newly formed claws underneath the mound of pillows. The sounds of fabric ripping were muted by the panting and moaning of their frenzied love making. He tweaked her nipples and then her clit and she came quickly against him. He followed right after her, utterly spent. Lowering himself to the bed, he wrapped his arms tightly around her.

"I don't think I have any more energy." Her voice was deep and raspy. Sexy as hell.

Kade slowly and methodically rubbed circles on her stomach and hip, her soft skin still glowing with their exertion. "We should rest and then I'm going to take you again. How does that sound?" He smiled against her hair when her body shivered against him, even though he had already pulled up the blankets over them both.

"Mmm. Okay. I think I can do that." Her words slurred with sleepiness.

He laughed and they both fell asleep.

He woke thirty minutes later and found himself wrapped around Mel's lush and delicious body. His cock was pressed up against her ass, and he was ready to take her again. Mmm. This was one of the most memorable nights of his life, and he knew that is wasn't quite over yet. His palm was pressed against her stomach and he slid it slowly up to grasp her breast. She gasped and rocked into his hand and against his cock simultaneously.

"Kade." Her voice was hushed and sounded barely awake but he caressed her breast while rocking against her. He licked and nibbled his way up her neck and chin while pinching her nipples. She gasped in surprise when he tweaked them harder and bit the junction between her neck and shoulder, without leaving the mate marking he so desperately wanted to leave.

She buckled against him as he slid his hand down to her pussy and pressed a calloused finger on her clit. "Melanie. You must be so wet for me. I am going to sink my cock into your pussy to make you scream my name again. Does that sound reasonable to you?"

Mel could only nod in response while she came against his hand and he entered her in one stroke, burying himself to the hilt. She screamed his name once more while still riding the peak.

"That's exactly what I wanted, Mel. And now when I do this I am going to play with this little puckered hole back here." He took her juices and spread it on her anus. He slowly played with her and entered just one digit to the knuckle.

"Oh God, Kade! Oh my God! Yes!" At first she tensed at the sudden and unfamiliar intrusion, but then fell back and relaxed so his finger could slide fully in. "Did I hurt you?" He would do his best to never hurt her.

"Oh Kade. Please don't stop. Please." She was gasping and her words were choked but not forced. His soon-to-be-mate looked mused with those rosy cheeks of hers like she had been fucked over and over again. His lover was a vixen and she would be his. He kissed her hard, fucking her mouth with his tongue when he entered her again fiercely. They continued on until they peaked and came crashing down together in a series of pants and gasps. They lay together for a moment before he extricated himself from her and rose to get a warm wash cloth. He cleaned them both up quickly before getting back into bed and pulling her into his arms.

"Get some sleep and we can talk in the morning."

He kissed her brow but heard no response as she was already peacefully asleep. He held her in his arms and whispered into her hair, "and soon baby, you are going to be my wife and my mate. No running. Just hope." He just needed to tell her that. Oh, and the fact that he was a hundred year old werewolf that wanted to bring her unsuspecting into his world. No problem there.

# CHAPTER 5

Melanie opened her eyes to the early morning sun, pleasantly sore and tired. She blinked once and then again, as images from the previous night assaulted her mind. Kade was so unique and new. He touched and pleasured her in ways she didn't even know could happen outside of the movies. She blushed as a shiver raced down her spine at the thought. His warm, muscular arm draped around her stomach and hips in an almost possessive nature and it made her smile. He was still there. Their lovemaking lasted up through the night and into the early morning, rocking against one another in the throes of ecstasy. During the brief moments between, they spoke of their lives and dreams. Kade was open and honest in most respects. He also seemed to be hiding something from her, but if she were honest with herself, she wasn't surprised. They were only going to be together for one night. Now that night was over. That was the premise of their blind date – there were no promises, no obligations. Now it was morning and even though she could have basked in his warmth forever, she needed to get up and get out of there before she lost anymore of her heart.

And oh how she'd lost it. Kade's actions spoke of kindness, yet he could be aggressive when needed. The man was gorgeous and amazing in bed. And he was also going to walk right out the door without her. Taking part of her with him. She took a steadying breath, slipped from his arm and out of bed, and wrapped the sheet around herself. Kade moaned and scooted closer to her edge of the bed as if missing her. *Wishful thinking.* She leaned down over him, and took in the beauty of his sculpted features, brushing a lock of his dark brown hair from his forehead.

*Gawd.* Leaving him would kill her. Missing him will be worse.

As she continued to look at him, a tear in the fabric in the corner of her eye made her pause. She narrowed her focus and moved one of the pillows.

Were those claw marks? What the hell?

There were long gashes in the sheets and mattress. Her breath quickened and she took a step away.

"Don't be afraid, Melanie. I can explain." Kade's deep voice was gruff with sleep.

"Explain what Kade? What the hell happened to the mattress?" She took another step away from him.

Kade slowly rose from the bed as if trying not to scare her. Too late, she was becoming pretty damned scared.

"It's going to be okay, Mel. I know I should have told you sooner but I can explain everything." Kade stood to his full height in all his naked glory and said in a calm and collected voice, "I am a werewolf."

Melanie laughed out loud at his announcement, yet even to her own ears it verged on hysterical.

*Seriously? Who does this guy think he is? Why not just announce he's a senator or something? That would be more believable.*

"Werewolves don't exist."

Larissa's words came back to her in full force and Kade's outrageous statement began to sink in.

*Just remember to keep an open mind. He really is quite sweet and won't bite. Well, only occasionally. And only if you want him to.*

Wait. Did Larissa know what Kade was? Why didn't she tell her? Pain and hurt exploded through her. Why would her best friend do this?

"You bit me?" Horror skirted up her arms, her neck. What did he do when she was sleeping?

"What?" Alarm and confusion blatant on his features. "No, of course I didn't. I would never do that without your permission."

"So you would bite me? Oh my God." Her chest heaved. He was delusional and she was alone in a room with him.

"Mel, baby, listen to me. I would never –"

"Werewolves aren't real." Yes. Keep saying that. Let him know his delusions were not going to scare her away – too much. She would get him help and then leave his fine ass and be safe. Good plan.

"Then explain the claw marks, Mel. Yes, I am a werewolf. But I wouldn't hurt you. I won't *ever* hurt you. Werewolves do exist and we have for a long time. But I'm just like you, Mel. I breath, I eat, I love. I just happen to turn into a wolf every once and awhile." He gave her a small smile that comforted her slightly but she was still hesitant. She couldn't give into his dementia, could she?

Something from the previous night suddenly came back to her.

"Your eyes. I thought it was just a trick of light, but last night, they glowed didn't they?"

Kade let out the breath he held. "I hoped you didn't catch that. Sometimes they glow when I am aroused or letting the wolf take over. I didn't want to scare you away last night."

"I still don't know if I believe you. Can you show me? Or do you have to wait for a full moon or something?" If all else failed, she was a chemist. A scientist. She needed analytical data. Proof. Melanie didn't know if she wanted him to be able to turn into a wolf right in front of her or for him to say he couldn't and it was just an elaborate hoax.

She pinched herself and it hurt. Nope. Not a dream. Dammit.

"No we don't need the moon to change. We do feel its pull more the fuller it is but I can change anytime. Are you sure you want me to change? I don't want to scare you."

"Too late, Kade." She said wryly. "But I don't want to believe you. Prove it."

"Okay."

Sure, Kade, like anything would come of this.

Standing right before her, his bones contracted and changed, fur sprouting from beneath his skin. He crouched lower and soon there was a slightly larger form of a real wolf with dark brown fur with a strip of white down his nose.

"Shit!" She stumbled back and her legs ran into the couch behind her breaking her fall.

"Oh my God. You are a werewolf. But how? Why? What?" She could barely put rational thoughts together. The science behind such a transformation boggled her mind. How did this happen? What else was out there? This idea completely went against every logical thing she had ever known and learned.

"Kade? Can you hear me? Do you understand me?"

The wolf - Kade – hesitantly approached her while bobbing his head up and down, like a nod.

"Can I touch you?" She raised her arm to put out her hand and Kade came up and let her fingers run in his fur. It was course but with a soft undercoat. She rubbed his head for a few minutes and then sat back against the couch.

Kade went back to the edge of the bed and changed back to human form.

His skin took a slightly sweaty sheen, as if he had been running but other than that he looked the same.

"Does it hurt?"

"Only slightly, but I was born this way so I am used to it. Those who are changed say it hurts more at first. But over time they get used to it and the pain recedes. I can't change too often or I run out of energy though."

"Is it still you when you are a wolf? Did you hear me?"

"I can always hear you and yes it's still me. But sometimes I let the wolf take over so he can run and enjoy the outdoors on the hunt."

"You should have told me."

"I know. But I was just worried that you would run. But there is nothing to be afraid of. Once you meet the others you will see that."

"Others? Wait, what do you mean that I will meet the others? I thought this was just for one night." Her voice was beginning to sound panicked again.

"I want more than one night with you. I want hundreds of years with you, Mel."

"What? How old are you?"

"One hundred and five."

Oh yes. Just state a number like that without emotion. *Gawd.*

"So you are like immortal or something?"

"No, just long lived. And once we're mated, you can be too."

"Mated? Kade, you need to slow down. I feel like I am missing a few things here."

"Sorry, I know I am going about this horribly but I just don't know a good way to explain. Yes, you are my mate. It's a feeling my wolf has and I, as a man, agree. I want us to be able to live long lives together. I know we just met but this is the way of the wolf. It's fate."

The jumbled thoughts swirled in her confused mind. "I thought you were with another woman before. You said it didn't work out. What did you mean?" The idea of fate was foreign to her and he couldn't be telling her everything.

Kade sighed before answering. "Yes, there was a woman before. But no, she wasn't my mate. Not like you. You're different." Mel let out an indigent huff. "When my wolf and I scented Tracy, that was her name, we thought she had the *potential* to be our mate. Fate had other ideas though, because her true mate was another. I'm happy about this, Mel. In fact, I wasn't that upset when I lost her. Not until you, did I know what it meant to find my heart and my other half."

"But how do I know? I'm not a wolf, Kade and I don't know if I want to be one. I don't have a wolfy feeling telling me that you're my mate." She paced around the room trying to collect her thoughts. "I do have feelings for you – I do. More than I should for just meeting you last night. But does that make you my mate and I yours?" She shook her head and blinked away the tears that were forming in her eyes. "I don't know if I want to live forever. I hardly even know you. I was thinking you were just going to leave after last night. This is too much to deal with. I think I need to go." She started toward her bags before Kade stopped her by gently touching her arm. His callused palm still sent shivers down her spine, but she ignored them.

"Don't go Melanie. Please stay." Looking down at his golden bronze skin resting against her paleness brought images from last night into her head. She shook off his hand, along with the memories.

"I can't Kade. This is too much." She quickly got dressed and collected her belongings.

"Then at least let me drive you home or get your number. I know I went about this all wrong, but we are destined for each other. I *want* to be with you. Please." Kade followed her around the room but kept his distance as if trying not to scare her any more than she was.

"You can give me your number but I need some space Kade. I don't know what to do. I just need to get out of here. I'll call you when I can think straight. I promise." Looking into his eyes, she tried to convey how much she wanted him and how honest she was trying to be.

Mel hesitantly walked toward him and stood on her tip-toes to kiss under his chin. His cheek showed the faint shadow of stubble and was rough against her lips. He lowered his head and took her lips in sweet and longing filled kiss.

She broke away before he could become more passionate and convince her to stay because of his body – that wasn't the way to get things done.

Mel took the paper that he had scrawled his number on and went to the door.

"I will call you, Kade. I promise."

She walked out the door and took one last look over her shoulder. Kade looked so lost and forlorn standing naked and alone in the center of the room, but when she looked into his eyes she saw something else. Determination.

# CHAPTER 6

M elanie's heels clicked across the linoleum, echoing in the empty lobby. The teardrop crystals from the lighting fixtures twinkled in the early morning sunlight. She paused, collecting her thoughts. Ironic. She stood by the same chair that she sat in and contemplated if she were making the right decision in going on this date. Now she was back, still struggling with her choices. An empty laugh escaped her. What a mess.

Her emotions ran wild. Fear bounced with happiness at the thought of Kade. A drop-dead gorgeous man wanted her for life, but why? Confusion and doubt settled it, seeping away any happiness. What Mel really wanted to do was run back upstairs, push away all of her emotions, and leap into Kade's arms. Yet, what did it mean to be mated to a werewolf?

Why the hell couldn't he have just been a nice *human* guy? Why was her life so fucked up?

"Melanie? Ms. Cross? Is everything okay?" A familiar deep voice broke her tumultuous thoughts.

The manager who walked her to her table last night stood by her elbow, a concerned expression on his face. Lance. Lance Morse. That's right.

"No. Yes. I'm fine. Just trying to get my bearings." It was then that she remembered what she was wearing – or rather not wearing. Still dressed in her black, lacy mini-dress, wrinkled from its time on the floor and her Fuck-Me pumps, Lance didn't have to guess what she did the night before. Her hand trailed up to her hair. Oh God. She must really look like she was just fucked, plucked, and made over. Heat infused her cheeks as mortification set in.

"Is there anything I can do to help? You took a cab in, correct? Would you like me to call one for you to get home?" Wow, she couldn't believe he remembered how she arrived. But she supposed that this was a nice hotel and the manager must know everything.

"Oh, if it's no trouble. I just want to get out of here quickly." She needed to leave this building before she lost her nerve and went back upstairs to the man who claimed to be her mate. Kade and his delectable body and apparently very sharp teeth.

Lance's gaze sought hers, his brow furrowed. "On second thought, I'm on my way out. Why don't I give you a ride home, save you the cab fare?"

Mel's eyes widened. "Oh, no. A cab will be fine."

The manager placed a warm hand on her arm. "Consider it part of the service. It's really no trouble, you look like you could use a friend to talk to. Let me help."

Too tired, worn and feeling used, she forgot to care about the potential dangers. She nodded. What the hell, she already slept with a stranger. Why not take a ride from another one. Truly risk fate.

After finishing whatever he needed to do, Lance led her to a tan sedan and opened the door for her.

Mel slid into the soft leather and released a sigh. She was running from a werewolf. An honest to God werewolf of the paranormal nature. Yep, she was certifiably insane. To top it off, she was in a car with a man she didn't know rattling off her address. She needed a shot of tequila, a deep sleep, and a number for a therapist. In that order.

The ride was quiet if not comfortable. Lance didn't speak, but generally seemed concerned for her well being. She couldn't think about the man she slept with though. Kade, in all his muscular glory, occupied her mind. His number sat in her bag, imploring her to dial. Would she?

"We're here." Lance's voice startled her.

Mel looked up at the small, plain townhouse she called home. Ordinary. Much like herself. This is who she was – not a werewolf's mate.

"Thank you for the ride. Do you want to come in for some tea?" Manners dictated an invitation that tumbled from her mouth before she thought.

A slow smile spread across his face. "That sounds nice."

Inside, Mel started a pot of hot water and took out two clean mugs.

"I have Earl Grey and orange zest."

"Orange sounds good. I don't need the caffeine. I've been working all night." He grinned, and for the first time, Mel noticed he was quite handsome and in her house. Alone. What was she thinking again? Oh right, the traumatic experience of a werewolf telling her she was his mate took her rational thoughts and put them in the garbage disposal.

This must be a dream. Why else would the chemistry wiz sleep with a man, and then go home with another. A hysterical laugh burst from her mouth.

"Melanie? Are you okay? No, I know you aren't okay."

Mel kept laughing, tears streaming from her eyes. Why wouldn't this night end?

"Melanie, I have something to tell you. I think you should just sit down."

Lance's calm, serious tone made her laughter cease. *Oh God, what now?* She sat on her couch, hot tea warming her hands.

"I don't know how to say this. But I am just going to say it," Lance nervously spoke.

Mel could only nod.

"Melanie. I'm a werewolf. You are my mate. I know you met Kade, and from the smell of it, you could be his mate too. But I want you to choose me. I know I am not Heir to the Pack, but I could still provide for you. Protect you. I don't want to fight Kade. I want you to choose me."

Lance's pleading eyes were the last thing she saw before she promptly passed out.

****

Kade stood naked in the room he shared with Mel for a full ten minutes, watching the closed door, before finally moving. She left.

*"Duh, Romeo. You let her go. You didn't follow her. What kind of Alpha-to-be are you?"* His wolf growled, and clawed to the surface.

Dammit. He wasn't going to argue with his inner half. Mel had to choose him. He wasn't going to force her and take away her decisions. He did that daily as Pack Heir, making decisions for them. His mate would be different, free. That was what he always dreamed, of a partnership, and he would be damned if he changed his mind now. Mel was a gift from fate and he wanted her by his side.

Kade quickly threw on his clothes from the night before. They held the faint smell of Mel. Honey and vanilla. A shudder passed through him. She would choose him. She had to.

He grabbed his keys and wallet from the dresser and left the room. As he walked through the lobby, he paused. A faded scent of oak and wolf. Someone from his pack – but who? Kade couldn't place it, but it didn't matter. They weren't confined to the den and could go where they pleased. However, the scent was mingled slightly with his favorite honey vanilla.

A growl rose in his throat, but he tempered it. No, it was just a coincidence. It was a large lobby, scents could mix together all the time. Assured that all was well, he left to his car to drive home where he could collect his thoughts and wait for a call. Because if he didn't have hope, there would be no absolution. No reason.

# CHAPTER 7

The smell of fresh pencils and wood shavings filled Kade's nose. The grey stroke of lead on paper looked like a series of lines, but together, they would eventually morph into a building – a home. He planned, he designed, he drew. He was an architect. That was his day job and way of earning a living anyway. Though he loved it and needed the feel of fresh paper beneath his fingertips, it was not his only duty. The blood of the Jamsesons ran through his veins and with it the weight of generations of responsibility. He was the Heir. A title placed on him at birth. As the first son of the Alpha, he carried the strength of history and memory. The Alpha's soul was connected to those of his Pack. His father could feel the presence of every one of the Redwoods – old or young. As the Heir, he too could feel their souls, but to a lesser degree at this time. With that connection came power and authority. From a young age, Kade knew that one day the decisions and fate of his entire Pack would rest on his shoulders. And yet, at this moment, not a single wolf mattered to him.

His mate walked out on him.

And he let her.

Why was that again? Oh yeah, his insane idea that his mate deserved a choice – free will. When he first learned about mating, Kade made his own decision. Whoever his mate, she would chose her own fate – not him. As Heir, he did enough of that for others constantly. Kade refused to do that to his life partner – his wife.

*A true Alpha wouldn't have let their mate walk away.*

Kade ignored his wolf. Animalistic instincts were the reason he got into most trouble anyway.

"Are you going to tell me what the hell is up with you?" His younger brother, Jasper, didn't startle him. He was a werewolf for fuck's sake, and Jasper's loud footsteps on his front porch alerted Kade to his brother's presence the moment he was there. Though as Beta of the Redwood Pack, Jasper purposely stepped heavily as not to sneak up on him. Their family was close enough, that some things, like warnings before invading their privacy, was just nice.

"I'm fine."

"Sure, that's why you are hiding in your home, scribbling away on your workstation, ignoring my calls. What happened last night?" Jasper sat on the stool next to him. Damn. There was no way he was getting out of this. For no matter the power seeping through his pores, Jasper was just as stubborn and took care of those he loved and vowed to protect.

"I went on a date. It ended. I am back." *Oh, and I found my mate, indulged in the hottest sex of my long lived life and then let the blonde goddess leave me naked, alone in the room. Oh, yeah, not much.*

"Okay. We're getting somewhere." Jasper grinned. Bastard. "How did the date go before it ended?"

45

"You may have set me up on the date, but that doesn't give you the right to play teenage dream with me, bro. We're not sixteen-year old girls and I didn't go out with the quarterback of the football team. Fuck off."

Jasper clasped his hands together and spoke in a high pitched voice, "Oh but Kade, you must tell me more, tell me more. Like did he have a car?"

Despite his ill mood, Kade burst out laughing. "Dude, you are so not Sandy or a Pink Lady. And you need to watch more TV so you can get more recent pop culture references. *Grease*? Really?"

"I've been busy. Between finishing that complex on the outskirts of town and dealing with the daily needs and wants of the Pack, TV and movies are the last thing on my mind. But you're changing the subject. What happened with Melanie? I can smell her on you, so I know it went at least somewhat well." Jasper's fist punched him on the shoulder, knocking the pencil from his hand. Damn persistent wolf was like a fucking Labrador sometimes, never giving up until he got attention. Jack-ass.

"Fine. We had sex. A lot of sex. Mind your own fucking business."

"I don't need details of that, pervert. I want to know how the actual date was before you went to the sheets. Seriously, I don't match make for a living, bastard. I am the Beta, I take care of my family, my own. And since Tracy, and frankly before Tracy, you have been on your ass doing nothing but work for the Pack or for the company. You needed a break from that, Larissa and I thought Mel and you would be perfect together. At least that was what Larissa thought, I only suggested to her that you needed to get laid. Damn witch wouldn't tell me anything about

46

your girl except give me that picture of her to give to you."

Okay, apparently Jasper was in a talking mood. Rare, and decidedly annoying. Fuck.

Kade let out an exasperated sigh. Jasper wasn't going to let this go. "The date went great actually. Melanie is smart, gorgeous, attentive and innocent. We ate, I talked, we went to the hotel room that you guys so graciously reserved for us. That's it."

Jasper merely lifted a dark eyebrow.

"I'm not talking about the sex." *The really mind blowing, wolf howling sex.*

His brother snorted. "What happened after the sex, moron?"

*More sex. And then some cuddling and some talking. And then some more sex.* He really needed to get his mind off of that. But it was so good, the way her face would blush when she came, calling his name. The feel of her wet heat clenching around his cock. And that's enough of that.

"Shewasmymate."

"Huh?"

"Melanie is my mate." There the words were out. And yet, no relief came. Just shared misery.

Suddenly Kade was airborne as Jasper pulled him into a deep, brotherly hug.

"Damn. Larissa knew what she was talking about. Your mate? That's awesome!" Jasper's smile was so contagious, it almost broke Kade's gruff exterior. Then, just as quickly as his brother's exuberance appeared, it was gone. "Wait, if you found your mate, then why are you here alone, looking like someone kicked your puppy? Is it because she is human? Because if you let her go because you don't think she is good enough for the Heir of the Redwood pack, I'm going to kick your fucking ass."

"Do you really think I'm that much of a pompous, entitled jerk?" Kade's muscles, flexed. Dumbass little brother thought it was okay to come in to *his* home and thrash him? Oh, he would show him who was Heir – Alpha in training.

"Well, look what happened with Tracy," Jasper's eyes widened as he spoke her name. Oh yeah, brother, you screwed up.

"This wasn't anything like what happened with her – and you know it. Don't fucking bring that clusterfuck of a situation up again." Anger raged through his system. This was not the same thing at all. He didn't want Tracy, and she left. Kade truly craved Melanie, and she left. See? No similarities.

*I don't understand you. How could you let our mate leave us?*

Again, Kade ignored his wolf. He would probably regret that later on their hunt. But he wasn't in the mood to justify his decisions.

"I'm sorry, Kade. I know Tracy is in her own realm of selfishness. I'll quit coming to my own conclusions. What happened with Melanie last night?" To his credit, Jasper actually looked contrite and generally interested.

Kade sighed. Jasper was his Beta, he relied on his brother more than any of his others. He should be able to tell him anything, rely on him for advice. That didn't make it any easier.

"Melanie and I did, um, complete part of the mating." Heat crawled up his neck. Yep, he was officially a teenage pup.

Jasper merely gave him a goofy grin. Ass.

"Well, you know." Kade took a deep breath, he was the fucking Heir. *Use big words dumbass.*

"We made love, our souls began the process of joining. But I didn't mark her, I wouldn't do that without her permission."

"Of course, Kade. You never mark your mate without a full understanding of mating. That's the first rule of it. Go on."

"I know you've never felt the urge of mating once you catch their scent," a shadow passed over Jasper's eyes, but Kade continued, "damn, it took almost all of my control not to shift. I couldn't use my full strength because she is so fragile, so my energy had to go somewhere, at some point my claws shifted. I was just so intense. I couldn't stop myself."

"Did you hurt her?" Jasper's voice was calm over a dark tone.

"No! No. I didn't. I have more control than that. But I did tear up the sheets and Mel noticed. I couldn't lie to her Jasper. I woke up and she's freaking out about the rips in the linens and I told her everything."

"Everything?"

"I blurted out like an idiot that 'I'm a werewolf.'"

"You didn't."

"In those exact words. I didn't lead up to it or try to make her feel better. Fuck. What was I thinking? Telling a human woman, my other half, that I'm a fucking werewolf? No wonder she laughed and thought I was crazy."

"Kade, what else did you do? Because I have a feeling this isn't the end."

"I proved it."

"How did you prove it Kade?" Jasper's voice had a nervous edge to it.

"I changed."

Jasper burst to his feet. "Are you fucking kidding me Kade? You change into a mangy wolf in front of her and you wonder why she isn't by your side?"

"I'm not mangy. I'm a fucking awesome wolf with a full coat." *Yeah, good comeback Kade.*

"So not the point, oh mighty Heir."

"Fine. I turned, she freaked. I turned back, she freaked some more. Then I told her my age and we were mates and we will be together for our long lives."

If Jasper's mouth hung open any wider, it would literally hit the floor.

"Don't say it, I know I didn't act with the most sense or grace."

"Kade, brother, you didn't act with *any* sense or grace. What the hell were you thinking? Let's get past the whole 'I turned into my wolf in front of a human and told them all of my secrets' thing, which by the way is against almost every code you know and uphold as Heir, thing. What happened when you told her this?"

"Well, she told me I was crazy and then she said she was crazy too. Then she let me give her my number and she said she would call, before she left the room."

"Damn."

"I'm pretty sure I lost my brain somewhere during the night though. I'm not a kid, Jasper. I know how to have a decent conversation, but I just don't know. Mel's honey vanilla scent turns me in knots."

"Honey vanilla?"

"Not the point, Jasper."

"What? It's the first substantial thing you have said about her. What are you going to do?"

Kade sighed. What would he do? She left him and he let her.

*You'll wait for her and welcome her. It's fate, Kade. She will come.*

Kade smiled at his wolf's basic idea of a nonbasic concept.

"I'm going to wait for her, Jasper. She will come to me – she has to. Its fate. I'm going to do all I can to make our home here for her though, in the meantime. When she does come, it will be to a place she can fit in and be happy. That's the least I can do."

"That's a great idea Kade. But why don't you go for her?"

"I can't. I promised myself as Heir and especially when I'm Alpha, I would not force my will and law on my mate. Melanie needs to make her own decision."

"If that's what you think is best."

"It has to be Jasper, it just has to." Because if she didn't call him, he would be lost.

# CHAPTER 8

Melanie's head throbbed. Her eyes slowly cracked open to see her living room ceiling. Was that a cob-web? She should really get up there to clean that. Wait. Why was she lying on the couch?

Oh yeah, her mental breakdown and the fact that werewolves apparently bred like bunnies.

"Thank God, you're awake."

Mel stiffened. Lance. Another self-proclaimed werewolf. He was still there. For the love of God, please don't try and prove it the same way Kade did. Don't panic. Just slowly get up and find a weapon – or call the police.

"Melanie? I won't hurt you. You're safe with me. I promise."

The crazy man – no, beast thing – said he wouldn't hurt her? And just how exactly was she to believe that? Yeah, silence seemed to be the best thing at this moment.

A cold, wet trickle trailed down her neck. Oh gawd. Was it blood? Did he decapitate her while she slept? *Okay Melanie, get yourself together. You wouldn't be breathing and talking to yourself if he took your head.* Unless he made her a zombie. Wait, were there zombies? A shudder ran through her.

A hand shot out and messed with something on her head. *Please, don't kill me.*

"Oh, are you cold? The ice I put on your cut is melting."

*Oh thank God, not blood. Just melted ice.*

"When you passed out, you hit your head on the table. You're going to have a rather large bump on your hairline, but I think you'll be fine." Lance's voice carried a thread of worry and care. Dammit, apparently werewolves are thoughtful.

"Please don't touch me." See? That was nice and calm.

Lance's face fell and he stood back. He looked like a kicked puppy. Mel snorted. Sometimes she cracked herself up.

"If that's what you want, Melanie. I'm sorry for blurting everything out like that. I'm just nervous." Mel gave him a good look. He did look cute, but in a best friend sort of way. Nothing like Kade.

Kade.

Her mouth salivated and her womb clenched as memories of the night before flooded her mind. They shared the best sex of her life, and then he ruined it by coming out as a monster of the night.

Lance's nostrils flared as a shudder racked his body.

Oh shit. Don't animals have a keen sense of smell? That's what she remembered from reading that romance novel Larissa gave her. Well, this was embarrassing.

"It's okay Lance, really. Just tell me what's going on. Why do you think I'm your," she swallowed hard, "mate?"

"You smell."

"Excuse me?" Well, just when she thought the guy was cute. She was gonna kick his ass.

"No. No, that's not what I mean. You smell perfect. Like honey. I swear." If Lance backtracked any farther he would be out of the house. Well, that sounded like a good idea.

"Lance..."

"My wolf scented you and that is how I know we are mates. At least the potential to be one..."

Now why did this conversation sound familiar?

"Lance, stop. I've already heard this from Kade."

"Kade. Right. About that, I know he thinks you can be his mate too. I mean, I..." Lance's ears blushed red.

An uneasy feeling settled in her stomach. "How did you know that exactly, Lance?"

"Um, well, I walked by your room this morning and heard your fight. I didn't mean to intrude, it's just werewolf senses, ya know."

Oh, she was beginning to.

"Lance, I don't think I'm your mate. And frankly, don't you think it's a bit rude to tell me this the morning after I find Kade?" She really just needed this guy to leave so she could think about Kade. Gawd, she already missed him. Yearned for him.

"I know it's regrettable that you already slept with the pup, but he didn't mark you so, things can be circumvented."

Egotistical bastard, wait... "Pup?"

"Kade's about fifty years younger than me, a boy in comparison. If you chose me you could have a man."

And that was it.

"Lance, you need to leave. Now. Thank you for the ride and the possible concussion, but you need to go."

"Melanie."

"Go."

The man backpedaled, practically running from her home.

What a night. She finds the perfect man, sleeps with him and then he informs her he's a werewolf. Then another man helps her and says the same thing. Two mates. She needed a drink and a friend. Mel walked to the phone to call Larissa. It was her fault she was in this mess, and she could get her out of it.

"Kade and Lance? You're one fucking lucky lady!" Larissa squealed before wrapping her arms around Mel.

"Didn't you listen to anything I said? They're werewolves. Kade changed right in front of me."

"So?" A genuine look of confusion crossed her friend's face.

"What do you mean 'so'? Are you telling me you knew they were wolves? That you know of this whole other world and didn't tell me?" Mel knew her voice shrieked, bordered on hysteria, but she didn't care. Seriously, this was too much to deal with.

"Mel, stop acting like a drama queen. I swear you've been spending way too much time with your nose in the hydrocarbons to look at anything else. Yes, I knew. I'm a witch."

Mel's head began to throb, her vision growing dim. No. She shook her head. One fainting spell was enough for the day. This wasn't the 1800s for Newton's sake.

"A witch. Like toil and trouble and smoking cauldrons type of witch?" Too late, Mel realized she might have offended her best friend. Crap. Maybe she was Wiccan.

Larissa merely laughed. "Is Hocus Pocus the only taste of witchcraft you've seen? Don't get me wrong, I love Bette Midler, but that's not what I am. I do have magic, but I'm also more in tune to the Earth. Mel, hon, there's a lot out there that you've never seen, but it's time to grow up, but on your big girl panties and open your eyes."

"What I need is a drink." *Maybe a whole lot of drinks. Like a barrel.*

"I brought the whiskey for your morning tea. Don't worry, babe, I know you. But after I give you a smidge, we need to talk."

"Fine."

Larissa prepared the tea while Mel sat and closed her eyes. Now that Lance was gone, the enormity of her situation began to sink in. She left Kade in the room so she could think. Did she want to change her life and be a werewolf's mate? Did she truly believe everything in front of her eyes?

"Mel," Larissa's stern tone pulled her from her worries. "You need to call Kade. You need to tell him what Lance said." A cautious look passed over her face. "Mel, this situation is more dire than you think. This is not only about you and your decisions. If you can't make a choice, they'll be forced to fight."

"A fight? Over me? That's fucking idiotic. If I don't want either of them, then they need to fucking walk away. Be a man."

"Mel, they aren't men. They're werewolves. There's something else you need to know." Mel wasn't sure she wanted to hear this. "Neil's one too."

"You're mated to a werewolf?" And just when she thought this day couldn't get any stranger. *Yep, the wolves were definitely multiplying in full force.*

"Yep. And I'm in a constant state of bliss."

"So that's how you know the Jamensons?" Things were starting to click in place.

"Yes, the Jamensons are the ruling family. Kade, is the Heir, first in line to be Alpha."

Mel knew the power running through his veins, felt it when he pounded into her. The strength in his hands when he gripped her tightly, yet the control in his almost gentle touch.

"So he's the big cheese. What does this have to do with your dire circumstances? Why do they have to fight?"

"It's tradition. The thing is Mel, Kade's already been through this before."

"Tracy."

Larissa quirked a brow. "I see he's told you a bit. Well, then I'll make this the unedited version. That bitch Tracy, dangled her perky breasts in front of Kade and his best friend, Grant. Then she claimed innocence and confusion, letting the men fight for her. That woman sure does love attention. Well, Kade really didn't want her – not like I'm sure he wants you. I can tell these things, sense them. But he's the Heir, so he had to fight. So he did, partially. Most of us suspect he gave up so Grant could have her. Good riddance. Fate must be a real temperamental bitch since Kade seems to be in the same predicament. That is, if you can't make up your mind." Larissa leaned forward, daring Mel to do just that.

"Why do I have to make up my mind? When I said yes to this overnight date, I said yes to dinner and maybe sex. Not a life altering wolfy fight."

"I didn't think to put it in the fine print, sue me."

"Fuck you."

"No, I think that's Kade's – or Lance's – job." Larissa didn't smile, but pushed the cordless phone

AN ALPHA'S PATH

toward her. "If you don't have the guts to call him, call Jasper. Here's his number."

"Larissa, I still don't know why they need to fight. I'm human, not a wolf. This isn't my problem."

"Melanie Cross. Stop being a selfish ass. It's time you grew up and took your nose out of your precious theories and science. This is affecting lives. Plural. Get over yourself."

Angered and a bit hurt, Mel glared at her so called best friend. "Larissa..."

Larissa held up a hand, cutting off her response. "Call him."

58

# CHAPTER 9

Kade stood back and smiled. Pride swelled as he dusted off the last of the eraser shavings. Finished. He spent the morning and most of the afternoon designing a preliminary sketch for the add-on to his home. A present for Mel. His home currently was a bachelor's nest, with heavy, chunky furniture and dark colors. The three-bedroom cottage most likely contained enough space, but Kade wanted to add more to it – to make it *theirs* not *his*.

Shit, since when did he become such a sentimental pup? The strength of his mating urge must be detrimental to the brain. If only his Mel would walk through the door. That would make everything better.

*Yes, so you can mount her and mark her. Perfect.*

Kade snorted at his wolf. Yeah, life didn't quite work that way. But his wolf could always hope.

The door crashed open, signal of Jasper's arrival. Tension and worry evident on his brother's features. This couldn't be good news.

"What is it?" Fear for his family, Pack, *Melanie* left a bitter taste on his tongue.

"You're not going to believe this."

"Tell me." Kade took a step toward him, urging him to continue.

"I need you calm, Kade. You can't go all Alpha and tear shit up."

Frustrated and nervous, he flipped Jasper off. "Fucking tell me."

"Melanie called," Jasper held out a hand before Kade could respond. "Like I said, Melanie called me. I don't know why she didn't call you directly, other than the fact she feared your reaction."

"What do you mean my reaction? Fucking get on with it."

"Seems you weren't the only wolf Melanie met last night."

Scents of oak and wolf flooded his memory. *Fuck.* Why didn't he follow up on the trail, rather than believing everything was okay? As Heir, he never left things to chance – except with Mel. *Fuck.* His wolf clawed to the surface, anger coursed through his veins.

"Who?" One word. One question grunted, pulled from his throat.

"Lance Morse. A low level wolf who manages the hotel you two stayed at. When Larissa and I booked your room, we didn't think anything of it. I'm sorry, Kade."

"Did he touch her?"

"No, I don't think so. Melanie is fine, Kade. But he took her home." Kade growled. *That fucking wolf thought he could care for his mate?*

"Kade, Melanie could be Lance's mate too."

Rage swept through his system. Blood pounded in his ears as Kade let out a gut-wrenching howl.

Not again.

He thought he was done with this indecision and fighting shit when he gave up Tracy. Was fate cruel enough to repeat his pain? Apparently so. *Damn!*

A hand on his shoulder brought comfort.

"Kade," Jasper's voice pulled him to the present. "We'll do what we can, but Mel doesn't know what to do. I don't think she wants this." Jasper sighed, pity in his eyes. "You know what must be done."

Yes. He knew. It was a familiar and acidic concept. If there were two potential mates, she would have to choose. If she couldn't – he would fight. Again.

And, fuck he would fight. Kade's wolf was already in love with her. The man was well on the way of following head over feet behind him. He and Mel shared a connection, even if she chose to deny it. The circle where he would fight for his heart called to him. He was the Heir, he would do what was right – what was just.

"Call the circle, Jasper. Lance and I will meet at the center. The victor will hold Mel's heart." It would be him. His wolf whimpered and growled. It had to be him.

\*\*\*\*

Mel watched as the trees passed in a blur. That's how her life in the past two days felt anyway. One event or person caught for a moment before falling into shadows – leaving but a memory.

A snort escaped her. Apparently, meeting two werewolves claiming to be her mate and breaking open her world to the paranormal let her poetic juices flow. All aboard the crazy train.

"So, where are we going? Or is this more cloak and dagger, secret society stuff?" Larissa wouldn't tell her. Her supposed best friend merely threw her into the passenger seat of her car and drove. She didn't even ask. Pushy witch.

"We're on our way to the Redwood den. It's deep in the forest." Well, Kade did say he lived on the outskirts of Seattle. "The Pack's lived there for over a millennia. It is deeply entrenched in Pack magic and history. So, don't be an arrogant ass and fuck it up." Larissa didn't let her gaze off the road, but her tone indicated a raised brow and no nonsense. Stern witch.

"I don't want them to fight over me. I just want to go to work and forget all of this." Even as she said it, pain ebbed through her. She knew she couldn't – no, wouldn't – forget Kade. His very essence imprinted on her soul. But was one night worth giving up everything she worked so hard for? How could one man – no, one werewolf – be enough for that? Kade's world eluded with violence. Hell, they were on their way to watch two grown men fight for the right to claim her. How Neolithic was that?

"I swear to all that is magic, Melanie Cross. This isn't about your closed minded human rules. This is something far greater than you – tradition. You don't want to choose between Kade and Lance? Fine. But then they have to fight in the Pack circle. Get over it." Apparently, Larissa crossed the threshold of being nice and understanding and entered the world of bitchiness. If Mel wasn't so confused, she could start to really like this side of her best friend.

"I sound like a sulky teenager, don't I?"

"You're more angsty than Edward Cullen on a sunny day."

Their laughter filled the car, releasing the ball of nervousness that churned in her stomach during the ride. No matter what she did, there would be a fight. Resigned, Mel took a deep breath.

A non-descript wooden arch signaled their arrival to the den. Larissa drove a bit further, nodding at the guards at the entrance. After a mile or so of dirt road, they finally stopped in front of what looked like a visitor center.

Really? What would be in there? *Please* feed the wolves?

A tall, built man opened the front door, walking toward their car. He looked slightly taller than Kade, with darker hair. But there was no mistaking the similar features and the fact he possessed the same jade eyes.

Oh, how she missed those eyes.

"That's Jasper, Kade's brother." Larissa's voice made her blink. Those Jamenson parents sure do breed sexy men.

Mel shook herself, bringing her attention to the striking woman following Jasper. Long blue-black hair fell past her shoulders and blunt bangs enhanced her features. This woman was easily the most beautiful woman she had ever seen. Again, her eyes reminded Mel of Kade. Damn, their genetics were a medical marvel.

Larissa opened her door and Mel followed suit. The cold mountain air tickled her nose. Inhaling, she sighed. The air smelled cleaner – crisper.

"Larissa, it's good to see you again." Jasper bent down and kissed her friend's cheek before turning to her. "Melanie, it's good to finally meet you." He smiled a sad smile. "I wish it were under better circumstances, but it doesn't make it any less true." Kade's brother lifted her hand to his lips, lightly brushing it. Though Jasper was very attractive, Mel felt no flutters of arousal. Apparently, Kade ruined her for others. *Damn wolf.*

"This is my sister Cailin." Jasper nodded toward the beauty, but the woman didn't acknowledge her.

"Cailin." One word on a growl and his sister bent her head, though Mel still saw a trace of defiance in her eyes.

Really? Bowing in submission? This is why she didn't want to be a part of this. She would belittle herself for no one. Enough of that happened during grad school, she was through.

"Ignore my sister. She's in a mood."

"Our brother is about to fight – maybe to the death – because this little blonde human refuses to make a decision. Excuse me if I don't welcome her with open arms." A viscous scowl turned her porcelain face into a menacing landscape of beauty.

"Excuse me? I'm sorry if I'm more enlightened than you, but I don't see a reason to fight over me."

"Oh, in that we agree." Cailin smirked.

"Okay, you may be a bitch – in every sense of the word – but don't fuck with me little girl." Who did she think she was?

"Stop it. Both of you." Jasper's voice commanded them both to obey. Surprisingly, Mel did.

"Let's just get this over with."

Jasper sighed. "Before we head to the circle you need to know a few things. Yes, they will meet in the circle over the right to mate with you. That is our custom – our ways. Please do not disrespect us and voice your detrimental opinions in our place of worship." He looked her in the eyes and Mel felt the beginnings of shame sweep over her. *Damn.*

"Kade and Lance will fight in the circle until one gives up – or one dies."

Mel's heart clenched. "To the death?" A whisper.

"Yes, Mel. To the death." Jasper's tone held no argument. "Are you sure you cannot choose?"

No words came. Lance wasn't an option. Not one bit. But was Kade? She wasn't ready to decide. How could she?

She could only shake her head.

Jasper let out a sigh before continuing. "You cannot interfere. You will watch and then you will let the winner come to you. Once they do – that is up to the two of you."

"I don't have to go with them do I?" Not that she didn't want Kade, but was this binding?"

"It's your choice once the circle is set and a victor emerges." Jasper checked his watch, "It's time to go."

Mel's heart raced as they walked toward the grassy circle surrounded by weathered stones. She didn't want to watch this. How could this be happening?

A glance across the circle took her breath away. Kade. He stood bare chested, muscles gleaming, and barefoot. His hair blew loosely in the wind, touching his shoulders. Just under three days passed and yet she missed him. She fell a little bit in love with him the night they shared together, but she didn't know if that was worth giving everything up. Losing her humanity. There wasn't enough time to think. Everything was happening too fast.

Her lover walked toward them on steady steps. For a man about to fight for his life, there was not a hint of nervousness. His face was blank of emotion except the slight sadness in his eyes. Was it sadness for her? Or the upcoming match?

"Kade." Nothing else mattered. The words she tried to string together in the car to say to him were gone. Though she didn't know her future, she wanted him to bend down and press his lips to hers.

Kade merely quirked the side of his mouth in a sad smile before lifting his hand to her face. He brushed her brow, trailing down to her cheek. His warm, calloused fingertip sent shivers through her.

But he didn't kiss her.

Too quickly his warmth left her. Did he not want her? Mel glanced down at his clenched fists and released a sigh. He wasn't as unemotional as he tried to show.

What was wrong with her? Her tumbling and confusing thoughts gave her a headache and hurt her stomach. Whatever happened here tonight would set the course of things to come. Now she only needed to make up her analytical mind. She needed more data, more time. But her heart screamed at her.

She was making the wrong choice.

# CHAPTER 10

Kade inhaled the mountain air threaded with the anticipation of the gathering crowd. An eerily familiar chill crept up his spine. *Damn, how could I be doing this again? What did I do to deserve this?*

He didn't know if he was speaking to God or his wolf, but neither answered. It appeared no matter what, he would be alone in this fight, and maybe for the rest of his life.

Despite his mind telling him not to, he risked a glance at Mel. *Damn.* It wasn't his imagination. Even with the worried scowl on her face, she still looked amazing. Her long blonde hair flowed in the wind, whipping about her face in small gusts. His hands fisted as he fought the urge to go over to her and brush a lock behind her ear.

Dammit, he was doing this for her. For them. Doubt clouded his mind. Did she even want him? Or was she like Tracy? Desiring another man, but without the backbone to say no to the Heir of the Pack.

Kade shook his head, dispelling the inner fears assailing his mind. He needed to focus. Lance stepped into the circle, a smirk of confidence on his face, yet fear in his eyes. *Huh?* Lance was a low-level Pack member. There was no way Kade could lose to him. That explained the fear, yet why the smirk?

"Kade." Lance's deep voice echoed through the circle and the noise of the Pack hushed.

"Lance."

"Men," his father's voice cut through their rising tension. "You're both here in this place of magic to battle, man against man, flesh against flesh, for the right to mate Melanie Cross." His father turned his head toward Mel, forcing Kade to do the same. She stood wide-eyed, frozen.

"Melanie Cross, do you acknowledge either of these men? Do you choose and stop this fight?" His father's voice boomed toward the crowd.

She shook her head, and Kade's heart plummeted. It didn't occur to him until right then that he was actually hoping she would choose him. What did he expect? One night and she would fall madly in love with him? It didn't matter that that's what happened to him.

Kade looked into Mel's eyes. Fear, yet pleading radiating from them. Without blinking, he turned from her toward his opponent. The smirk didn't leave.

"Why are you smiling?" Curiosity pulled the words from him.

"You've lost before pup, and she never said no to me. Why would she want the politics that come with your job? With me, she has more options."

Uncertainty attacked him. Dammit.

"Watch your back Lance. I will fight with everything I have. Mel's worth fighting for. Remember the power I hold that comes with my 'job'. Don't fuck with me." Kade growled the last part, wiping the smirk off the jackass's face. Good.

"Men, stand ready at the center. And begin when I tell you." Sadness threaded his father's voice. No father wanted to see their son, especially their first-born, fight, maybe to the death, for a mate – twice.

Kade planted his feet, the soil smooth against his bare skin. Clad in only an old pair of faded jeans, his mobility was the greatest it could be without being naked. Much as he would like to walk around nude in front of Mel, the others may frown upon that. Plus the whole dangly bit issue during a fight – not a good idea.

Lance stood four feet across from him, mimicking Kade's stance. Though all werewolves were required to go through fight training as adolescents, not all Pack members were adequate in it. Kade knew every single wolf in his pack. Because he was Heir, he also felt each of their souls. Lance wasn't a fighter; he was a schmoozer, a prick.

*Kick his hairy ass.*

Ah, nice to see his wolf didn't leave him completely alone. Kade inhaled, letting his wolf rise to the surface just a bit. A warm golden glow appeared on the ground in front of him. Good, his eyes were lit, time to get this shit over with.

"Now," the Alpha commanded.

Lance jumped first, attacking with his right, leaving his left flank open. Amateur. He ducked and sank his fist into his opponent's side. The other wolf howled in pain but rolled with it, before kicking at Kade. He moved to the side, narrowly escaping the blow and spun to punch Lance in the face. Bones crunched under his fist as Lance's nose broke. Again, the other wolf screamed but didn't quit.

They fought, scraped, and hit, neither backing down. Kade risked a look at Mel. Her hands were in front of her, balled together with tension. Her eyes were wide with panic yet she was still beautiful. His.

He wasn't surprised when the punch hit him square in the jaw as his attention was focused elsewhere. Pain radiated through his cheekbone and lower mouth as his teeth crashed together. *Fuck.* Kade spun and returned the blow. Lance's head snapped back, the blood oozing from his lip mixing with the congealed blood from his nose.

Kade needed to end this. Mel was his. Not this fucking wolf who couldn't even fight to protect her. His wolf snorted and clawed in agreement. *Good.* He growled, letting his Heir power radiate. Lance blanched. *Fucking wolf better fear him.* Kade punched with his right, flesh in to Lance's cheek, breaking the bone. Then punched with his left, ribs bruising underneath his fist. Lance gasped, a green hue flowing over his skin, before falling to the ground.

Though a fight to death might be expected, Kade needed a yield. He would not kill another man in front of Mel. Fear already wafted from her skin, and he didn't want to add to it. Kade knelt by the fallen wolf, the crowd's cheers silenced. He placed his palm on Lance's neck, cutting off most of his air-flow.

"Back down, Lance. You cannot win this. I refuse to kill you in front of her."

Recognition flashed in his eyes. *Yeah buddy, I love her and I could kill you. Give up.*

Lance lifted his chin, bearing what little neck he could. It was over.

The crowd cheered. Their Heir won. Victorious. But Kade knew it wasn't over. He may have won the battle, but he would not force his Mate. No matter the traditions.

The audience quieted as Kade walked toward Mel. His heart pounded in his ears. This was by far scarier than the fight he just left. He loved her. What if she said no? What would he do if she left?

Kade stood in front of her. The sweet honey vanilla smell masked by her fear and pain.

"Mel?"

\*\*\*\*

The brutality of the fight left Mel speechless. This was not humane. No, this was barbaric, animalistic. Her fault. Before Kade walked into the circle to fight, she knew she was making the wrong choice. Why did she let them fight? Why didn't she love Kade enough to leave everything behind she has known and worked for?

Even as she thought about it, she knew the answer. While she attended school, choices were made for her, paths laid and followed without resistance. Yet, now she held the decision. The power to follow her own life, her own path. No one could take that from her. She'd known Kade for less than a week. Spoke to him for less than a day. If he had merely given her time to decide before, the outcome may have been different. But not now. Confusion racked her brain. Time wasn't an option, so the decision would break her heart. Already, she felt numb.

"Kade," her voice broke. "I..."

"Leave us." Startled, Mel looked around. The crowd dispersed quickly and quietly. Some still held curiosity, but most looked upon Kade with pity.

Whether it be for her humanity or they knew her answer, she didn't know.

Drawing on the little courage she had left, she spoke, "Kade, I can't." Pain flashed in his eyes, but he didn't speak. "This isn't my life. I can't give up everything for a man I don't know. Kade, we don't know each other. You may have a wolf to guide you, but I only have my experiences."

No one spoke for what seemed like an eternity. Then Kade bent down and brushed a lock of her hair behind her ear. Her breath hitched as he leaned further to touch his lips to hers. His hand still in her hair, he pulled her to him, kissing her with a desperation she thought was only hers. Their tongues clashed, lips hungry and eager. Finally, Kade released her.

"If that is your decision, I will let you go. I love you, Melanie Cross." He lifted his arm as if to touch her once more, but let it fall.

With one last look, he pleaded with her, but she didn't know what to do. He left the circle, taking her heart with him.

# CHAPTER 11

K ade sat on his porch, a beer in his hand.
Though his metabolism would burn off the
effects quickly – he needed to feel nothing.
Numb. Anything to get his mind off the fact that he
was mateless after meeting two potentials. Mateless
after two meetings in the circle. Mel left him.

*You let her leave, you fool. Why didn't you tie her
up and keep her here. I'm sure there's something you
could've done to pass the time while she makes the
right decision.*

Kade snorted at his wolf's attitude. Though an
image of Mel tied naked to his bed-posts flooded his
mind. *Fuck.* He shook his head. She left. That
delicious fantasy would never happen.

Footsteps sounded on his driveway, altering Kade
to an unwelcome guest.

"Hello Kade, you look like shit." The sickly sweet
voice pinched his nerve endings.

Tracy.

Tall and curvy, her body lent itself to many pup's
wet dreams. Long chocolate brown hair flowed to her

ass, hours of work evident in its perfection. His body didn't react. She wasn't Mel.

"What are you doing here? Shouldn't you be with your mate, Grant?" Fuck, that sounded jealous. No, he wasn't jealous of Grant. One look at Mel and Kade knew – Tracy wasn't for him. No, he was jealous of what Tracy and Grant shared. What he lost when he let Mel walk away.

"That's not a very nice greeting to someone you loved now is it?" She batted her eyes and pursed her lips. Typical, she needed something. What, he didn't care. He just hoped she would leave so he could wallow in misery with his beer in peace. Was that too much to ask?

"I never loved you, Tracy, you know that. I thought we could have something because of our wolves, but you didn't want me either." Pain made him honest and slightly bitter, but who the fuck cared.

Tracy huffed. "Fine, Kade. Be an ass. But you are the fucking Heir of this Pack and you need to act like it. It was bad enough you were going to mate that human, but then you *let* her leave? I'm glad I picked Grant. You're nothing."

A growl slipped from his lips and she cowered in fear. Tracy's wolf possessed almost no strength, yet she was a bitch. Kade, however, didn't give a shit. He wouldn't move from his perch for anyone but the blonde who left him.

"Leave Tracy."

"No Kade, I won't. I'm sorry for saying that, but I need help."

"Go."

"But its Grant, he lost his job and..."

"Go."

"Kade." Her whiny voice pleaded. Kade wanted to throw up.

"Tracy, I don't care about you and Grant. If you have a problem, go see Jasper. That's his job. But leave me the fuck alone. You wanted Grant? You have him."

"And you have nothing." Tracy's sneer only confirmed his own shortcomings. It wasn't anything new.

"Goodbye, Tracy."

"I'm glad that human left you. You aren't even worthyof that piece of shit."

Kade leapt off the porch and had Tracy on the ground, gasping for breath before she could blink.

"You may call me names but you will not dishonor Melanie. She is mine."

"But..." He pressed down harder on her windpipe.

"I love her, Tracy. You will respect her."

Her eyes widened and she nodded before Kade released her. She scrambled up, not bothering to wipe the dirt from her dress and ran.

*You chose the right woman, Kade. Tracy isn't worth anything. Mel will come back. She will see reason.*

Kade let out a pathetic half-laugh. No, Mel made her choice. Kade was just the one who had to live with it.

\*\*\*\*

Ben and Jerry's Karmal Sutra ice cream was manna. The creamy caramel and chocolate fudge ice creams surrounded a thick column of caramel goodness. Mel sighed in ecstasy as she let another spoonful melt on her tongue, the flavors cascading in an almost orgasmic symphony.

And this was as good as it got. Ice cream and the Discovery Channel on a Saturday night. No men or sex for her. She was the fucking idiot who walked away from her mate and left him. Now she faced four hundred freshman three days a week teaching them general chemistry, though they could care less. When she wasn't banging her head against the chalk board explaining once again that energy of light is inversely, not directly, proportional to it wavelength, she was again stuck behind a lab bench. With her new title she now called the shots but she still didn't have a passion for it. She really didn't give a crap about the radioactive nuclides and alkali metals in different silicates and soils. She'd lost her passion. No, not lost, she'd left her passion with Kade.

Her door opened without an announcement and Larissa strode in, an angry look on her face. After the match, and her dismissal of Kade, Larissa drove her home in a silence that scared the shit out of her. Her best friend wouldn't even look at her, nor speak. When they arrived at her home, Larissa sat there, a sad look on her face and waited wordlessly for Mel to leave. That was the last time she saw her and it'd been almost a month. Mel braced herself – this wouldn't be good.

"You pathetic human. You are sitting here eating fucking ice cream and watching the god damn TV? What the hell is your problem?"

"Larissa..."

"Shut up, I'm not done yet. You left the perfect man for you because you didn't know him? Why couldn't you have just talked to him? Is that such a foreign concept? For such a smart girl, you sure do make the worst decisions."

Shame flooded her. She knew she made the wrong decision, but how could she go back to him? She left and walked away. He didn't want her back. Why would he?

"I know you're miserable. I can feel it pulsating from you. Why are you still here?" Larissa sat down on the couch in an inelegant plop, exhaustion, and clear bewilderment on her face.

Mel broke down in gut wrenching sobs. She knew she was an idiot, but she couldn't go back.

"Oh baby." Larissa moved to her side and enveloped her in her arms. Warm scents of apple pie and earth filled her nose. Mel dug deeper, salty tears running down her face, staining her best friend's shirt.

"Shh, it's okay. We can fix this." Her witch crooned in her ear, comforting her.

"I don't think I can, Larissa. I think I screwed up bad."

"Don't worry, just cry it out. We'll figure out something."

"But what if he doesn't want me?" Deep down that was her biggest fear. And if Mel were honest with herself, that was her fear all along. She lied to herself when she said it was about her job, her life. No, fear ruled her and said Kade would change is his mind and let her go. So she let him go first. Or worse, he would do the honorable thing and stick with her, but resent her through their long lives.

"Oh baby, he wants you. He's just as miserable, if not more, as you."

"Really?" Okay, now she was happy that he shared her misery. *Wow. Pathetic, much?*

"He's your mate."

Yes, he was.

# CHAPTER 12

She never called. A month passed and his mate didn't call. Kade knew he should have followed or begged her. But he couldn't. He kept to his own promise as Heir to not influence or force his will on his mate.

The past month clearly won for the hardest of his life. His wolf barely spoke to him and was grouchy as hell. In turn Kade acted like an ass to anyone who came within five feet of him.

His father, the Alpha of the pack, told him to get his shit together and stop moping about a woman. *Nice. Great parenting skills there.*

He threw himself into his work and designed his mate a home. Their home. She would come back. She had to. Once she came, he would start building so they could have a future together. If he lost that hope and let the stray thought of her not calling enter his head, he didn't know what he would do. Maybe go lone wolf, because he wasn't sure his Pack would tolerate his mood much longer. His heart ached for Mel. He could barely eat, and sleep was a far off concept.

The sound of a foot on a broken tree branch brought him out of his reverie and he turned to the source, ready to attack.

Honey and vanilla teased his senses.

Mel.

She stood in front of him, in light worn jeans and dark green sweater. His wolf howled in celebration.

"Melanie." A gasp along his breath. *Why?*

"I'm so sorry Kade," her eyes filled with tears and he fought the urge to wipe them. "I needed more time, but I shouldn't have left the way I did."

The uncomfortable silence grew heavy with tension.

"Why are you here?"

*Oh good job ass. Why aren't you welcoming her with open arms?*

"I called yesterday. Your father answered and told me where you were. He also told me you were acting like a shithead and I needed to come fix it. I think it was an order." She smiled wryly at him and he laughed at her.

"My father knew you were coming? What the hell? Why didn't he say anything?" He needed to kick his father's ass once his brain turned back from mush.

"I think he wanted it to be a surprise. Don't be mad at him. I am sorry it took so long for me to get my act together and not be an idiot. I'm sorry I left. I'm sorry you even fought. Lance was never an option Kade." Hope swelled. She wanted him, not that douche bag.

"I was so lost and confused at first and by the time I got my thoughts into something similar to a coherent pattern, I had so much planning to do."

"Planning?" he really needed to work on those one word sentences.

"Planning." She smiled and continued. "I had to quit my job and find a teaching position I liked near here. I know that I won't be able to stay there too long because I won't be aging and that might become suspicious but I still want to work for awhile. Of course if I become pregnant that might be another matter. Oh and will I give birth to puppies? Because frankly that scares the shit out of me." She smiled again and Kade lost it. His mate was moving here and talking of bearing his young. *Heaven.*

He couldn't wait any longer. He grabbed her and crushed his mouth to hers. He almost forgot her taste of sweet ecstasy. Her tongue fought for control against his as she rocked her body against him.

After however long they stood there tasting and touching each other, they finally broke apart gasping for breath.

"You're here. You are really here."

"Uh huh." She smiled brightly and his heart melted again.

"I love you Melanie. I am so glad you came. I made a house for you. Well not a full house, just the plans, but if you want to change everything let me know. I would do anything for you, my Melanie." He held her against him and breathed in her sweet scent.

"I love you too, Kade. I am sorry it took so long for me to get here. But I'm not leaving. I want you too much and I want to see your world. Teach me everything."

"My pleasure, mate, I will teach you anything you desire." He smiled wickedly and carried her off to his room. Melanie was here, with him. Their future together would intertwine, walking the same path. It was about time.

\*\*\*\*

Kade cradled her to his chest, the feel of his heartbeat against her cheek brought her home. No amount of job security or teaching could replace this.

"I love you Kade." She knew she already said it, but it needed repeating.

"I know."

Mel slapped his arm.

"Really? 'I know?' Who do you think you are? Harrison Ford?"

"Oh God, my mate makes *Star Wars* jokes. I think I just fell a little more in love with you." Kade set her on his bed – their bed.

Mel gulped. "I talked to Larissa about mating and she told me a bit." Kade looked down at her expectantly while stripping them both of their clothes. "I want you to mark me."

His eyes glowed as he growled. "That can be arranged." A guttural sound. His hands shifted, sliding up her bare skin sending goose bumps down her body. The cotton sheets below her cooled her overheated body, as he kissed her lips, then along her jaw down to her neck. She braced herself for the bite, but Kade lifted his head.

"Are you sure you want this?" Oh, how she loved this man, this wolf. Even now, he gave her options.

"Yes. With everything I have."

Kade moaned before kissing her, his tongue playing with hers. She fought for breath as his mouth trailed long her neck again, and gasped has his calloused fingertips brushed and pinched her nipples. He licked the crease where her neck met her shoulder and she shivered. Anticipation crawled through her. She felt his teeth elongate before they punctured her shoulder. The tension of her skin ebbed as his teeth slid into her skin.

Mel braced for the pain, yet it soon passed as a soft flow of love and sex flooded her. *Holy shit.* Kade's bite pulsated through her body, pinching her nipples and clenching her pussy. As he bit and growled, her climax neared. Kade bit harder once more and her control broke. Spasms of need and glorious warmth cascaded as she came. *Fuck, and he didn't even touch her down there.*

"Mine." One word. Yet full of possessive meaning.

Her mate removed his fangs as they slid back to their normal self.

"Yours." Her voice deepened into a raspy tone.

Still wet and swollen from her orgasm, the head of Kade's cock brushed her folds and she shuddered.

"I want you Melanie."

"Now. Please."

Kade, propped up on his forearms above her, kissed her softly. Gazes locked, he entered her in one quick thrust. She groaned as her walls clamped down on him. He practically whimpered, then reared back and slammed into her.

Each thrust brought her closer to completion as she lay underneath her mate. He reached down and drew circles around her clit and she shattered, him following soon behind.

"I love you Melanie."

"I love you Kade."

Though her path may be radically different than what she planned, here in Kade's arms, Melanie found her true destiny. Forever.

The End

*Next in the Redwood Pack: A Taste for a Mate.*

# A Note from Carrie Ann

Thank you so much for reading **AN ALPHA'S PATH**. I do hope if you liked this story, that you would please leave a review. Not only does a review spread the word to other readers, they let us authors know if you'd like to see more stories like this from us. I love hearing from readers and talking to them when I can. If you want to make sure you know what's coming next from me, you can sign up for my newsletter at www.CarrieAnnRyan.com; follow me on twitter at @CarrieAnnRyan, or like my Facebook page. I also have a Facebook Fan Club where we have trivia, chats, and other goodies. You guys are the reason I get to do what I do and I thank you.

Make sure you're signed up for my MAILING LIST so you can know when the next releases are available as well as find giveaways and FREE READS.

An Alpha's Path is the first book in the Redwood Pack saga. There are seven books and at least seven novellas in this world. Plus starting in 2015, the series continues with the Talon Pack.

If you don't want to wait that long, I also have my Dante's Circle and Montgomery Ink series going in full swing now so there's always a Carrie Ann book on the horizon! Plus coming in 2015, I have the Bad Boys of Haven! Wow, I'm tired just thinking about it but I can't wait.

**Redwood Pack Series:**
Book 1: An Alpha's Path
Book 2: A Taste for a Mate
Book 3: Trinity Bound
Book 3.5: A Night Away

Book 4: Enforcer's Redemption
Book 4.5: Blurred Expectations
Book 4.7: Forgiveness
Book 5: Shattered Emotions
Book 6: Hidden Destiny
Book 6.5: A Beta's Haven
Book 7: Fighting Fate
Book 7.5 Loving the Omega
Book 7.7: The Hunted Heart
Book 8: Wicked Wolf

Want to keep up to date with the next Carrie Ann Ryan Release? Receive Text Alerts easily!

**Text CARRIE to 24587**

# About Carrie Ann and her Books

New York Times and USA Today Bestselling Author Carrie Ann Ryan never thought she'd be a writer. Not really. No, she loved math and science and even went on to graduate school in chemistry. Yes, she read as a kid and devoured teen fiction and Harry Potter, but it wasn't until someone handed her a romance book in her late teens that she realized that there was something out there just for her. When another author suggested she use the voices in her head for good and not evil, The Redwood Pack and all her other stories were born.

Carrie Ann is a bestselling author of over twenty novels and novellas and has so much more on her mind (and on her spreadsheets *grins*) that she isn't planning on giving up her dream anytime soon.

## www.CarrieAnnRyan.com

**Redwood Pack Series:**
Book 1: An Alpha's Path
Book 2: A Taste for a Mate
Book 3: Trinity Bound
Book 3.5: A Night Away
Book 4: Enforcer's Redemption
Book 4.5: Blurred Expectations
Book 4.7: Forgiveness
Book 5: Shattered Emotions
Book 6: Hidden Destiny
Book 6.5: A Beta's Haven
Book 7: Fighting Fate
Book 7.5 Loving the Omega
Book 7.7: The Hunted Heart

Book 8: Wicked Wolf

## The Talon Pack (Following the Redwood Pack Series):
Book 1: Tattered Loyalties
Book 2: An Alpha's Choice
Book 3: Mated in Mist (Coming in 2016)

## The Redwood Pack Volumes:
Redwood Pack Vol 1
Redwood Pack Vol 2
Redwood Pack Vol 3
Redwood Pack Vol 4
Redwood Pack Vol 5
Redwood Pack Vol 6

## Montgomery Ink:
Book 0.5: Ink Inspired
Book 0.6: Ink Reunited
Book 1: Delicate Ink
Book 1.5 Forever Ink
Book 2: Tempting Boundaries
Book 3: Harder than Words
Book 4: Written in Ink (Coming Oct 2015)

## The Branded Pack Series:
## (Written with Alexandra Ivy)
Books 1 & 2: Stolen and Forgiven
Books 3 & 4: Abandoned and Unseen (Coming Sept 2015)

## Dante's Circle Series:
Book 1: Dust of My Wings
Book 2: Her Warriors' Three Wishes
Book 3: An Unlucky Moon
The Dante's Circle Box Set (Contains Books 1-3)

Book 3.5: His Choice
Book 4: Tangled Innocence
Book 5: Fierce Enchantment
Book 6: An Immortal's Song (Coming in 2016)

**Holiday, Montana Series:**
Book 1: Charmed Spirits
Book 2: Santa's Executive
Book 3: Finding Abigail
The Holiday Montana Box Set (Contains Books 1-3)
Book 4: Her Lucky Love
Book 5: Dreams of Ivory

**Tempting Signs Series:**
Finally Found You

# Excerpt: A Taste for a Mate

**From the next book in New York Times Bestselling Author Carrie Ann Ryan's Redwood Pack Series**

The scent of cinnamon and sugar danced on the air as Willow Delton heaved opened the heavy oven door to remove her prized cinnamon rolls. The plump, buttery pastries were baked to perfection, and she set them on the counter to cool. The only thing missing was her thick and creamy frosting, but that would have to wait.

Willow stood back and stared around her commercial grade kitchen. She'd started her bakery from scratch, and it had grown into a successful, albeit small, business. Incredible, really. She'd never thought the day would arrive when she finally had a place to call her own. She was right where she wanted to be. Her favorite part of the day was being able to meet one-on-one with her customers. She loved the looks on their faces when they bit into her temptations, that look of ecstasy not seen on this side of the bedroom door that flashed across their eyes.

Of course, that particular look as the result of a man was long absent from Willow's face. Too excruciatingly long.

She stood back and closed her eyes, conjuring the memory of her mystery man's face. The image that filled her mind made her forget the lack of human contact. The thought of his deep, husky voice tickled her spine whenever he spoke. Green eyes caught her in his web with only a glance. She'd fallen for a stranger and didn't even know his name. He'd come into her store every morning and ordered a cinnamon roll and coffee with only a few words. Then he 'd pay cash before lifting up the corner of his mouth in a semblance of a smile and walking out of her store. Was it strange she worried he'd keep walking and never return?

A bell's tinkle pulled Willow from her reverie and self-pity. As she turned to greet her customer, her heart leapt to her throat. Him. Her mysterious fantasy man. As she tried to regain her senses, she took all of him in. He had to be one of the tallest men she'd ever seen, easily over six and a half feet. The tight black T-shirt he wore hugged his biceps and cut into his muscular physique, while his broad shoulders stretched and strained the seams. His body tapered down to a narrow waist and hips as they met his thighs. His long legs she wanted to grip, encased in worn jeans lead to work boots. Hmm, construction perhaps? She glanced back up his body to his striking face.

He wasn't beautiful, but he did have a face most women would dream about. A strong jaw and cheekbones gave him an aura of strength, the kind of strength that would be protective. His hair was midnight black and long enough to brush his shoulders, however, today, a band held it back, showcasing his face more. He studied her, his green eyes calm and calculating. Willow let out a surprised gasp at the sexual heat radiating from him. Could she possibly be imagining things?

****

Jasper Jamenson fought himself as he walked into the bakery that morning. This would be the seventh week in a row he'd come here, every day but Sunday. And that was only because the damn store was closed. As good as the cinnamon rolls were, and they were little tastes of heaven, it was the woman behind the counter that brought him there every morning.

Following a particularly bad night in the forest on a hunt, Jasper had been pissed and hungry. Another wolf had tried to play a dominant game, forcing Jasper to hurt him. The stench of the other's defeat had remained on him, only angering Jasper that much more. The scent of the morning's freshly baked goods pulled him through the quaint and welcoming door, and the slender goddess who served him brought thoughts of a different form of servicing to mind.

Slightly above average in height – he would guess about five foot seven – she was the perfect height to settle against his body. For someone who owned and operated a bakery, she was as skinny as a rail. However, if he looked close enough he could see the telltale signs possible of curves. And with just a little bit of his help and pampering she would gain some well-needed cushion. No matter what, she'd look amazing underneath him. Her long, light brown hair curled in a bun on the top of her head. His fingers ached to pull out the pins and watch it tumble down her back. Hazel eyes sought him and begged for his protection. Damn, he was willing.

Her look made the wolf within him perk up and growl.

*"Mate? I want her"*. His wolf paced beneath the surface of his skin, calculating the best way to quickly claim their mate.

What his wolf spoke of was a possibility. There were only a few women in the world through time that carried the scent to signal the potential mating. Unlike his brother Kade, who had met two women recently that carried the scent, Jasper had never in his one-hundred and three years come across a woman who brought forth the mating urge. However, if all encounters were like this one, Jasper didn't know how others walked away. The urge rode him hard and he fought his wolf for control if only for a moment, something that hadn't happened since he was a pup.

He mentally spoke to his wolf. *"We are not ready for a mate. And a human no less. She knows nothing of us. If, and that is a big if, we chose her to be our mate, we will have to go slowly into this. I don't want us to scare her. But she is beautiful, no"*

His wolf growled in response.

*"Do you want to scare her away? Let's get to know her first, see if she is a good match, other than that incredible cinnamon scent. I'll talk to Adam and find out everything I can about her. I am the Beta; I cannot put my Pack in jeopardy."*

God, he really sucked at this. This time he needed to put on his big wolf panties and actually ask her out.

*"Then we could mark her."*

He snorted at his wolf. Yeah, that was taking it slow.

Jasper shook himself from his inner thoughts and looked into those hazel eyes. The spot of flour on her cheek begged for his hand to brush it way. He fought the urge. No need to freak her out. Her chest moved slowly, her small breasts rising and falling. The cinnamon scent of her filled his nostrils and he took a deep breath, the aroma going straight to his cock. The slight gasp that escaped from her kissable lips almost broke his control, and he fisted his hands to regain it.

"Good morning." His voice lowered an octave and became a growl. He cleared his throat and started again. "I come here every morning and I don't think I ever gave you my name. Let me rectify that." He closed the distance between them so only the counter separated them. "I'm Jasper Jamenson. It's a pleasure to meet you." He held out his hand in hopes of touching her skin.

Willow blinked up at him and seemed at a loss for words. Her lips opened slightly, begging him to lean down and taste her.

"Uh... yeah... I'm Willow Delton." She shook her head, gave him a small smile and placed her slender hand in his. He'd been right – her skin was incredibly soft and made him want to take a bite.

"Yes, I know, you own this place." He gave her hand a squeeze and released her.

"So, Jasper, do you want your usual?" The sound of his name on her lips hardened his cock. Without waiting for him to respond, she turned back to her work-table to ice her cinnamon rolls.

"Sounds good." He watched as her hands moved swiftly and confidently across the baking sheets. "What time do you get off?"

*"Smooth, Romeo. Why don't you just ask her to bend over the work table for you?"*

Ignoring his wolf Jasper continued, "I thought that we could grab a bite to eat tonight and go see to the arts fest they have running in town."

Oh dear Lord. Why didn't he ease into this?

"Oh, are you asking me out on a date?" She wrinkled her brow and looked utterly confused at the prospect.

"Yes, I am. I've been in here for over a month every morning, and as much as I love your food, I had an ulterior motive."

Surprise flashed across her face before her eyes lit up with excitement. "I've never been to the arts fest in town. I didn't want to go by myself and didn't have anyone to go with me." Her mouth snapped shut at her revealing statement.

Laughing quietly, he shook his head. "So what time do you get off?"

*"You really need to stop putting it like that; it gives me ideas."* Again, he ignored his wolf's sarcasm.

"I close at four and should be done cleaning up by five. It's only me here today so it's going to take me an hour to close."

"What do you say I come back at six and we go to dinner from here?"

Her smile almost blinded him as she nodded before taking off her apron. "Okay. Sounds good. Here's your breakfast." She handed him his black coffee and a small brown bag with a pink logo.

Taking everything from her hands, he set them down along with the cash to pay for it. Giving into temptation, he leaned over the counter to brush the flour from her cheek.

She jumped and a flash of alarm raced across her face.

Chuckling under his breath, he reassured her. "Just some flour. I'll see you at six, Willow." He grabbed his breakfast and walked to the door, taking one last look behind him at the woman who was his mate. He was one lucky bastard.

Whistling a jaunty tune, he walked toward his Jeep, unconcerned and happy while leaving his mate to do her work. The hairs on the back of his neck lifted, and his wolf came to attention. The street was empty but for a few people; nothing looked out of place. Jasper took a deep breath but didn't detect another presence. With one last look toward his slender brunette, he shrugged off the uneasy feeling and continued to his Jeep.

# Charmed Spirits

**From New York Times Bestselling Author Carrie Ann Ryan's Holiday Montana Series**

Jordan Cross has returned to Holiday, Montana after eleven long years to clear out her late aunt's house, put it on the market, and figure out what she wants to do with the rest of her life. Soon, she finds herself facing the town that turned its back on her because she was different. Because being labeled a witch in a small town didn't earn her many friends...especially when it wasn't a lie.

Matt Cooper has lived in Holiday his whole life. He's perfectly content being a bachelor alongside his four single brothers in a very small town. After all, the only woman he'd ever loved ran out on him without a goodbye. But now Jordan's back and just as bewitching as ever. Can they rekindle their romance with a town set against them?

Warning: Contains an intelligent, sexy witch with an attitude and drop-dead gorgeous man who likes to work with his hands, holds a secret that might scare someone, and really, *really*, likes table tops for certain activities. Enough said.

# Ink Inspired

## From New York Times Bestselling Author Carrie Ann Ryan's Montgomery Ink Series

Shepard Montgomery loves the feel of a needle in his hands, the ink that he lays on another, and the thrill he gets when his art is finished, appreciated, and loved. At least that's the way it used to be. Now he's struggling to figure out why he's a tattoo artist at all as he wades through the college frat boys and tourists who just want a thrill, not a permanent reminder of their trip. Once he sees the Ice Princess walk through Midnight Ink's doors though, he knows he might just have found the inspiration he needs.

Shea Little has spent her life listening to her family's desires. She went to the best schools, participated in the most proper of social events, and almost married the man her family wanted for her. When she ran from that and found a job she actually likes, she thought she'd rebelled enough. Now though, she wants one more thing—only Shepard stands in the way. She'll not only have to let him learn more about her in order to get inked, but find out what it means to be truly free.

Made in the USA
Middletown, DE
27 February 2018